Camp Timber View

Jason Deas

Ball Ground, Georgia, USA

3-Day Ranch Press

© 2011

Acknowledgements

Kaylen and Cara: Thanks for asking me to write a book for kids. I enjoyed every minute of it. I love you both more than you will ever know.

Sammie and Jackson: You two are awesome. When I think about you my heart flutters.

Karen: Thanks for letting me write another one. I love you.

Mom and Dad: My editors and my rock.

Carrie McAtee: Thanks for the "last read" and peace of mind.

"We are what we pretend to be, so we must be careful what we pretend."

Kurt Vonnegut, Jr.

Chapter 1

Reggie's older brother Ronald picked his nose on the couch as he watched wrestling on television. Reggie was supposed to be practicing the trumpet, but Ronald said his ears hurt from the awful honking noises that came out of the brass instrument. Ronald kept teasing him and asking if a sick goat had somehow broken into the house. Ronald told Reggie to go outside or he would practice his wrestling moves on him again. *One day,* Reggie thought, *I am going to show him what I think about his stupid wrestling and all the dumb TV shows he watches.*

Since his mom and dad weren't home from work yet, Reggie decided to go play outside. As he walked out onto the back porch he spotted Sally climbing up into the neighborhood tree house. The tree house sat in the vacant lot next door. A few years back, the house that used to stand there caught fire and burned mostly to the ground. People said old Mr. Robinson fell asleep in his bed with a cigarette that caught the bed on fire. He lives with his son now, and Reggie heard he quit smoking. A few months after the fire a bulldozer came and knocked the rest of the house down. Old Mr. Robinson never sold the lot so Reggie's dad and Sally's dad built the biggest tree house most kids have ever seen.

Four trees held the enormous tree house. The four trees had grown almost as perfect as the four corners of a square. A giant porch wrapped around the two story tree house. Inside, the first story's ceiling was high enough to stand all the way up. Not so much on the second story. Older brothers, sisters, and other big kids could not fit in there. Reggie and Sally called it the lookout or the safe box. It had a tiny window looking down on the lot below.

1

The first story had two large, open windows. In the middle of the floor was a hatch that could be opened and closed and this is where the ladder connected from the ground.

As Reggie climbed the ladder he heard a low, sad cry. Sally had somehow folded her body into a corner of the tree house, and she looked like a pile of sobbing clothes. Reggie hated to see her cry. They had been best friends since kindergarten.

"What's wrong, Sally?" Reggie asked.

Sally slowly sat up, and her black hair parted like curtains opening, revealing her dark eyes. Reggie could tell from the red around her eyes that she had been crying for a long time. Her little nose, which he thought looked like a rabbit's, was running down her lip and he took off his light jacket and offered it to her to wipe her nose. They were that good of friends.

When she finally stopped crying and snorting all over Reggie's jacket, Sally told him why she was so sad.

With anger now she said, "When school gets out, my parents are making me go to summer camp!"

"Summer camp?" Reggie asked in disbelief. "How long does that last?"

"All summer," Sally answered.

"What about us catching fireflies, swimming, riding our bikes to town to buy candy, and sleeping on the trampoline?"

"Not happening this summer," Sally said as she blew the last of her snot into Reggie's jacket. She handed the jacket back to Reggie and said, "Thanks."

Not thinking anything of it, Reggie tossed it out the window of the tree house and said, "Anytime." Reggie thought for a moment and asked, "How did all of this happen?"

"This is where it gets a little weird," Sally started. "I saw this huge golden ticket with my name printed on it sitting on the kitchen table. Mom saw me look at it when I came in this afternoon and picked it up real fast. She didn't think I had time to read it, and when I asked her what it was she said 'nothing'. Then, she gets on the phone with my dad. She went in the other room and shut the door, but I could hear she was all excited. When she came out she told me to sit down, handed me the ticket, and told me I had won a free trip to Camp Timber View for the summer."

"You won a trip?" Reggie said with disbelief. "You're eleven. Eleven-year-olds don't win trips!"

"They do now," Sally said. "Mom was holding a bunch of papers and told me she had to read all about Camp Timber View and sign some papers."

"Oh my geez," Reggie said as he held his hands over his cheeks. "What am I going to do without you? All Ronald does is watch TV and boss me around. Who is going to catch craw daddies with me and build dams down at the creek?"

Just then a voice cried out. It was Reggie's mom. "Reggie," she called. "I need to talk to you."

Reggie said goodbye to Sally and hurried down the ladder. He grabbed the snot filled jacket off the ground and dragged it toward the house, leaving it at the back door. Reggie entered the house and walked to the kitchen where he heard pots rattling and water running. These were the familiar sounds of mom cooking.

As Reggie entered the kitchen he saw the day's mail strewn out on the counter. Among the contents of the mail was a huge golden ticket that read, "Reggie."

Chapter 2

Reggie and Sally sat in Mr. Cain's fifth grade art class with lumps of clay in their hands. They studied each other as they kneaded the clay. As close as they were, Sally could not read Reggie's mind—it was a first.

Reggie knew the worried look on Sally's face had to do with summer camp. He smiled. He actually laughed a little out loud.

"What is so funny?" Sally asked.

"I got a golden ticket," Reggie said smiling.

"You did what?" Sally asked. "Oh my geez," she said with disbelief, realizing what was happening.

"I'm going with you," Reggie said. "Goodbye Ronald. Goodbye TV. Hello Camp Timber View."

As Sally processed the information a smile crept across her face. She was relieved. Someone who felt like family would be there all summer.

Still kneading the clay, Sally asked Reggie, "What did Mr. Cain say he wanted us to make?"

"He just said to use the slab technique," Reggie answered.

"Well, I guess I can just roll out a big piece and lay it over your giant head if I want to shape a salad bowl."

"Very funny. I think I'm going to make you an ashtray for your birthday," Reggie joked.

"Nice," Sally said, noticing Mr. Cain standing behind them.

Mr. Cain looked at them sternly, broke a smile, and asked, "Do you two comedians think you could talk and *work* at the same time?"

"Yes, Mr. Cain," they answered in unison. Reggie and Sally began slapping the clay back and forth between their hands again trying to get the invisible air bubbles out that Mr. Cain cautioned would explode in the kiln when fired, if not taken care of. Mr. Cain said it would destroy their pieces.

"Are you coming to my party Saturday?" Sally asked, quieter than before as she continued working. She glanced at Mr. Cain and he winked at her with approval.

"Yes, I'm coming. Am I going to be the only boy again this year?"

"No. I invited Roger."

"Is it going to be a princess themed party?" Reggie asked with a worried look.

"No," Sally answered, offended. "I'm too old for that."

"It was a princess party last year," Reggie argued.

"Yes," Sally agreed. "That was last year. It has been three hundred and sixty something days since then. Do you still sleep with that blue stuffed cat?"

"OK. OK. And no, I don't sleep with Bobo the cat anymore." Reggie *did* still sleep with Bobo the blue stuffed cat. He received the cat on his second birthday from his Uncle Jeff, and it had always been a security blanket to him. Trying to change the subject, as Reggie worked, he said, "I'm sorry, but I don't think your ashtray is going to be ready by Saturday."

"Shucks," Sally said, laughing.

On the playground at recess that afternoon, as Reggie ran from the affection of Mary Kate Gleason, he stepped directly in the center of the only puddle on the school grounds. The depth of the puddle swallowed his shoes up to his ankles, and luckily Reggie was wearing shorts. Already wet, Reggie walked to the center of the puddle to escape the giggling Mary Kate Gleason. She eyed the giant puddle as her delirium for Reggie quickly faded. Looking away from the puddle and scanning the play area, Mary Kate Gleason spotted another target and ran off laughing again in a frenzy of boy crazy giggles.

Reggie stood there seething. He did not see Sally approach from behind. She stood at the edge of the massive puddle smiling a wicked smile.

"Aren't you a genius," she said as he slowly turned around to view her tricky grin. "I'm sure Camp Timber View has a lake. Can't you wait just two more weeks?"

"You think you're funny don't you?" Reggie said with a little smile of his own.

"You have to admit," Sally answered, "this *is* amusing. I can't even see your shoes."

"Maybe I took them off and I am just cooling my feet," Reggie countered.

"But, you didn't."

"No, I didn't." Changing the subject Reggie asked, "Are we walking home together this afternoon?"

"Do I have to walk through any puddles with you?"

"No, smarty pants you don't. But we are going to cut through Mr. Jimmie's backyard."

"Oh come on," Sally said, suddenly frightened.

"You said you would on Friday and it is Friday."

"I thought you would chicken out," Sally said with her lip turning down. "Do you really think he shoots at kids who trespass on his land?"

Reggie had the tricky smile now and he said, "He does."

Chapter 3

Cracks began to run all over the sidewalk as Reggie and Sally neared Mr. Jimmie's street. He lived at the edge of town. The cracks began as trickles and tiny scribbles of lines. With each step they evolved and thickened. With twenty more steps, grass and weeds poked and peeked through the fractured cement. As the sidewalk ended, it didn't look like a sidewalk anymore but a concrete puzzle of broken rocks. It was as though the world started to crumble away the closer they got to Mr. Jimmie's land.

Mr. Jimmie lived at the end of a quiet dirt road. Both Reggie and Sally thought it was too quiet. Even the crickets and birds were scared of Mr. Jimmie it seemed. The sky darkened as a cloud passed in front of the sun. Reggie and Sally stopped to peer at one another. At the same moment a crow cawed with a loud call, and the two jumped and grabbed hands. They both realized at the same time they were holding hands, and they released their grips and began walking again pretending that the hand holding had not happened. The crunch of gravel under their feet was the only sound they heard.

There had been many, many stories about Mr. Jimmie. He was supposedly a millionaire, crazy as a fox, and the most truthful man in the world. It was the main reason most people were scared of him—he was blunt.

As Reggie and Sally neared the house, they began to notice the birdfeeders. They were obviously homemade, probably by Mr. Jimmie, and incredibly strange. A giant white one with four stories and many, many holes had "The Birdie Motel" painted on the side. They also saw one fashioned as a teepee, another as a houseboat, and another as a slice of watermelon; the open holes looked

7

like the seeds of the watermelon. Some of the birdfeeders were high in trees, some were on poles, and some sat along the fence posts surrounding Mr. Jimmie's ramshackle home.

A grey paint the color of camp fire soot coated the boards of the house that seemed ready to fall at the next gust of wind. The shingles atop the roof reminded Reggie of a dry lakebed he had seen once that was lined with dried and cracking mud. Sally, looking at the roof, imagined buckets scattered around the inside of the house to catch water when it rained. The screens covering the filthy windows all had cuts in them as if cats had used them for scratching posts. The porch looked like an abandoned recycling center. Jars lined the railing of the porch, and each of the jars seemed to hold something unique and disgusting. Cans, bottles, newspapers, magazines, and other odd collectibles filled the crowded porch. Reggie and Sally stood in disbelief that a man that supposedly had millions of dollars could live like this. A cow was also tied up to the porch.

Reggie's brother Ronald and his band of hooligan friends had once snuck up to Mr. Jimmie's house with their slingshots. They took small rocks and shot the cow in the hindquarters. It didn't really hurt the cow as much as it did annoy the animal. The cow thrashed around and made horrible noises that brought Mr. Jimmie out of his house to investigate. On spotting the boys hiding in the brush, Mr. Jimmie retrieved his shotgun, walked out to the porch, and fired one shot into the air—hence the legend of Mr. Jimmie and the infamous shotgun.

As Reggie and Sally crept across Mr. Jimmie's yard, they both held their breath with fear. The cow, still tied up to the porch, spotted them and eyed them wearily.

Behind them they heard a soft crunch of leaves and turned in unison to see Mr. Jimmie standing behind them.

Reggie and Sally froze with fear. Mr. Jimmie looked a mess. Loose skin hung from his thin face which was speckled with a patchy, white, stubbly beard. His eyes were crazed with confusion, and his body shook with nerves. Mr. Jimmie rolled his tongue around the inside of his mouth as if he were feeling it for the first time. He smacked his lips and looked as if he were searching for something to say as he eyed both Reggie and Sally.

"I know you," he said scowling at Reggie.

"No sir," Reggie answered, "I don't think you do." Reggie was terrified. His knees shook and once again he and Sally unconsciously held hands.

"You gave me the jelly," Mr. Jimmie said as his left eye blinked uncontrollably. He slapped himself in the eye with two quick pops and the twitching stopped.

"The jelly?" Sally questioned. "What jelly are you talking about?"

"I was walking home one day with my groceries," Mr. Jimmie began. He pulled a pair of glasses out of his shirt pocket and put them on upside down. "And I dropped my jelly," he said, taking off the glasses and putting them back in his pocket. "Jar busted on the sidewalk." He took out the glasses and put them back on, this time the right way. "Young feller here," he said, tapping Reggie on the head, "saw what happened. I was cursing and crying I admit. I love grape jelly." Mr. Jimmie ran his fingers through his tousled hair recalling the event. He took the glasses off again. "I set my other groceries down to clean up the broken jelly jar and this feller here," he said, tapping Reggie once again on the head, "handed me a brand new jar of grape jelly. He said he would clean

9

up the busted one, handed me my grocery bag, and sent me on my way."

Sally turned and looked at Reggie. "Oh yeah," Reggie said. "I remember that now. That was a long time ago."

"I never forgot it," Mr. Jimmie answered. "I never replaced your jar of jelly," Mr. Jimmie said. "Your mama must have wore you out."

"She didn't care," Reggie said.

"I'll replace it now," Mr. Jimmie said. He took off his left shoe and hopped on one foot toward the house. Once on the porch he took off the other shoe.

"Should we run?" Reggie asked Sally as Mr. Jimmie entered the house.

"I think that would hurt his feelings," Sally answered. "He may be crazy, but crazy people have feelings too."

"What if he just went inside to get his shotgun?"

"Get real," Sally answered.

Mr. Jimmie came out of the house, now barefoot, wearing a ladies hat. He did not have a shotgun or a jar of jelly in his hands.

"I don't have any jelly," he said as he approached the kids. "I want to give you this instead." Mr. Jimmie reached into his shirt pocket, retrieved his glasses, and handed them to Reggie.

"Don't you need your glasses?" Reggie asked.

"Oh," Mr. Jimmie said taking them back. "Wrong pocket." He reached into his pants pocket and pulled out a shiny, brand new miniature tape recorder. He handed it to Reggie who was stunned to see something like this come out of the broken down house. "And I got you this hat,"

Mr. Jimmie said taking the ladies hat off his head and placing it on Sally's.

With that said, Mr. Jimmie picked up the left shoe off the ground he had previously taken off and threw it on the roof of his house. He was laughing uncontrollably as he walked back into his house.

Chapter 4

The last few weeks of school flew by. Sally's party came and went and Reggie *was* the only boy there. Summer floated in with a mild, boring air until the morning the mail lady pulled into Reggie's driveway and blew the horn.

The couch, as usual, held Ronald who was flipping channels. He called to Reggie who was in his room constructing a Lego castle.

"Get the door, Reggie," he called.

"Who is it?"

"How would I know," Ronald answered.

Reggie took a break from the drawbridge he had been trying to construct to answer the door. Reggie peeked out of the window to see who it was as his mother had instructed him to do. You never answer the door for a stranger he remembered. As he peeked out he saw the mail lady, Ms. Heather. Reggie opened the door.

"I've got a box for you," she said to Reggie. "It has your name on it."

"Something for me?" Reggie said with surprise.

"Yes," Ms. Heather said. "The box has a giant golden ticket painted on the front."

"Oh," Reggie said, realizing where it must have come from. "I bet it is from Camp Timber View."

"Yep," Ms. Heather said. "I think that is what the return address reads."

Together, Reggie and Ms. Heather lifted the box out of the mail truck and carried it to the front porch. Once the box sat securely on the porch, Reggie thanked Ms. Heather for the delivery, and she wished him luck and a good time at camp.

Reggie ran to the kitchen, pulled a knife out of a drawer in the kitchen and walked back to the front porch. He sliced the tape from the top of the box and folded the flaps of cardboard back. The box was enormous. It was the kind of box Reggie would have turned into a fort a few years ago before the tree house was built. An army green trunk sat inside the box. The top of the trunk had a giant logo for Camp Timber View. Reggie wondered how he would get the trunk out of the box knowing Ronald would not help even if it was a commercial. He never moved from the front of the television. Instead of asking Ronald for his help, Reggie cut the four sides of the container and folded all the flaps down to the porch floor. With the flaps all folded down and the trunk exposed, Reggie noticed that one side of the trunk had a handle, and the other side had wheels. Reggie lifted the handle, pushed the front door open, and wheeled the trunk to his room.

The trunk had a latch for a lock, but it was not locked. Opening the lid of the trunk, Reggie's eyes sparkled as he viewed the treasures packed inside. Atop the loot sat a padlock. A twist tie looped through the U-shape of the lock attached to a piece of paper revealing the combination. Reggie sat the lock and combination aside. Reggie began pulling items out of the trunk beginning with long and short sleeved t-shirts bearing the Camp Timber View logo. There were seven of each in different colors. Reggie stacked them neatly on the floor next to the trunk. Shorts, sweatpants, bathing suits, and even pajamas followed. All of the items, Reggie noticed, had the Camp Timber View logo. Next came a backpack filled with a canteen, flashlight, a headlamp, binoculars, a poncho, two hats, a compass and batteries. Two more items remained in the trunk. Reggie eyed the army green sleeping bag first and then tossed aside the note hiding the final item. Reggie picked up the black carrying case and slowly pulled the zipper opening the protective holder. He reached his hand in and pulled out the most beautiful piece of equipment he had ever seen, a digital camera. It wasn't just any digital camera. It took videos, could shoot underwater shots, it had what seemed like a million different buttons that could do anything and everything. Reggie had never owned anything so beautiful in his entire life. This was not a kid's camera. This camera was top of the line, and Reggie could barely wait to leave for camp.

Chapter 5

Reggie waited on the front porch of his house, sitting on top of his packed trunk. The camp's bus was scheduled to pick him up at any moment. His mother and father waited with him. His brother Ronald was too busy watching television as usual.

"Don't forget to wear your sunscreen," his mother said.

"Mom," Reggie sighed. "You have said that at least two hundred times. I won't forget, but even if I did there are worse things than a little sunburn."

"Yeah," Reggie's father piped in. "He could drown, be eaten by a bear, get lost in the woods, or fall off of a mountain."

"Thanks Tom," Reggie's mother said as she shot his father a nasty look.

Clearing his throat, Reggie's father said, "Son, please wear your sunscreen." As he said this, Reggie's father gave him a secretive wink and a slight grin.

Suddenly a deafening boom filled the air and echoed through the houses in the neighborhood. A vehicle's exhaust had clearly backfired as it sounded like a bomb had dropped out of the muffler. Reggie along with his mother and father all turned their startled eyes to the top of the street where a loud grumbling began to rattle and bounce through their ears and into their heads. As they stared in the direction of the commotion, a purple double-decker bus rounded the corner and slowly headed toward Reggie's house. As the purple bus slowed to a stop in front of Reggie's house, they all noticed the Camp Timber View logo painted in log cabin brown. The driver shut off the engine, and the bus once again backfired,

15

reminding Reggie of fireworks and the fourth of July. The boom must have frightened Ronald off his beloved couch in front of the television because he came flying through the front door to see what all the commotion was about.

The family stood in silence and eyed the unmoving door of the bus. Reggie thought he saw the door twitch. His mother felt as if it may have moved an inch. His father swore in his mind it shook. Ronald had a notion it was stuck. And then, the door ever so slowly but surely began to move. One inch, two, three, four, it crept until the door stood fully opened. The family remained silent as they waited for someone to appear. Surely the bus did not drive itself. And then the driver emerged, and the strangest summer of Reggie's life began. Reggie thought he might have been a mad scientist. His mother felt he had escaped from the old folk's home. His father swore he was a retired superhero. Ronald had a notion he was dreaming. An older man, very tall, with stark white hair, giant glasses, dressed in a sports jersey, Hawaiian pants, and last but certainly not least—a yellow cape came into sight. He spoke in rhyme.

> "Reggie, Reggie, there you are
> We have to go, so so far
> Let's not waste one, one beat
> Get on the bus, take take a seat
> Dad will you do me one big chore
> Put Reggie's stuff through the back door
> If you'll do that with his trunk
> I'll have a camp counselor take it to his bunk
> Now give your brother hugs and your parents

kisses

We have to get started filling a summer full of wishes."

Surprisingly, Ronald did give Reggie a hug. Reggie kissed his mom, and she smothered his face with a bouquet of kisses, leaving traces of her lipstick on his cheeks. She told him she loved him five or six times. Reggie's father put his trunk in the back of the bus and gave him a loving hug with a sweet kiss atop his head.

"I love you Reggie," his father said.

"I love you too Dad," Reggie answered.

As Reggie was about to disappear into the bus, Reggie's father called and stopped him.

"Reggie," his father called.

"Yes Dad," he answered.

"Don't forget to wear your sunscreen," he said laughing with a tear in his eye.

"I won't Dad," Reggie said. "I won't."

A double-decker bus has two levels. They are used all over the world to transport people within cities and especially on long journeys. Double-decker buses are not often seen in rural Georgia, especially purple ones. Reggie was instructed in rhyme by the driver to sit on the upper level. The lower level was full of trunks.

As Reggie neared the top of the stairs he heard a giggle which he instantly knew belonged to Sally. Little did he know, she had been watching him out of the tinted windows of the bus. She had seen him with the nutty bus driver. She knew him well. He would never act like it, but he had been freaked out by the guy. He would need a minute alone, to gather himself. Sally scooted toward the window leaving a spot for Reggie and remained quiet. The driver cranked up the bus, and they pulled away as the purple double-decker bus once again backfired. Reggie waved to his parents although they could not see him through the tinted windows. His mother had tears in her eyes, and his father had his arm around her. Ronald was not there. Reggie decided he must have gone back inside so he didn't miss too much of his television show. Reggie watched them disappear in the distance and then turned his eyes to Sally. She smiled, but waited for him to speak first.

"That was weird," Reggie said. "Did the bus driver talk like that to you?"

"Yep," Sally answered. "He picked me up first. He has said the same thing to everybody. Believe me, I've been watching. He freaked me out too."

"Weird," Reggie said again, staring out of the window. He seemed to be thinking deep thoughts, so once again Sally left him alone. She knew when to leave him alone. After a mile or two Reggie pepped up and asked, "How far is this place?"

"I think it is about two and a half or three hours," Sally answered.

Reggie and Sally watched out of the bus window as the land turned from hilly to mountainous. The bus drove up some very steep inclines and rounded some extremely sharp curves. At times it seemed like the bus was hanging, suspended above nothing. The sky filled the background with a cloudless blue. A few birds glided on the wind in the distance, and the scenery brought a calm and quiet to the bus that lasted the entire ascent.

As the bus reached the mountain's peak it pulled into a large parking lot accompanied by a sign that read, "Scenic Overlook."

Reggie got off the bus looking for a bathroom. They had a bathroom on the bus, but the smell seeping from under the door kept him from going in. Reggie quickly found one and asked Sally to wait for him. Sally sat down on a rock ledge as Reggie ran into the facility tugging at his zipper. She watched all the other kids get off the bus and mill around. When Reggie came out he had a different look on his face, a look of relief. Reggie sat down next to Sally on the rock wall just as they heard the bus once again backfire. They both looked up to see the bus race out of the parking lot. The crazy driver had his head back, laughing like a madman.

Chapter 6

Before Reggie and Sally had a chance to comment on the bus leaving, their attention turned to the sky where they heard the roar of a low flying airplane. As they looked up they noticed little specks of color in the sky falling below the airplane. The colored specks were little parachutes guiding tiny packages to the ground. All the campers eyed the sky, wondering what the packages might contain. As they neared the ground, the children scattered under the many parachutes, each making their claim.

After catching a box, Reggie and Sally ripped them open. The other campers did the same. Each box contained a bottle of water and a riddle. The riddle read:

> Wisdom from Oz
> Take a part a guitar
> A valley opposite of life
> Hocus Pocus go home

As each camper read the riddle, a silence fell over the group. Moments like these made leaders. Sally looked around at the other kids and at Reggie. She counted eight other kids besides her and Reggie. The camp brochure said there would be about two hundred people at the camp, and she wondered if they all had to do this. She nudged Reggie and gave him a look that said, "What do we do now?" Reggie shrugged his shoulders.

"Alright everybody," Sally said in a loud voice. "I met some of you on the bus, but why don't we make a circle and everybody can say their name." They listened. Once in the circle Sally said her name and turned to Reggie. He said his and they continued this around the circle. When it came back around to Sally she said, "Let's make sure all of our notes say the same thing. I'll read mine and anybody tell me if their note is different." Sally read her note aloud and nobody said a word, which meant they had all received the same riddle.

"Who is good at riddles?" Sally asked.

"I'm pretty good at them," a boy with curly brown hair answered. "Riddles are easiest if you just take them one line at a time."

"Great idea," Sally agreed. "So, 'Wisdom from Oz' means what?"

A ponytailed girl asked, "Do you think they mean *The Wizard of Oz*, the movie?"

"It also is the abbreviation for an ounce I think," another voice said.

"My dad watches a show called *Oz*," came yet a different voice.

Reggie had been listening to the ongoing conversation as he looked around. He noticed the signs for a few different hiking trails. Each trail was marked by painted rings around the trees. A red ring circled the trunk of a giant pine accompanied by a sign that read, "Follow the red..." A different area had a large oak banded with green paint. The sign next to the tree read, "Follow the green..."

"Follow the yellow brick road," Reggie yelled as he began to search for a yellow tree.

"What are you thinking?" Sally asked.

"In the movie *The Wizard of Oz*, the good witch and the munchkins tell Dorothy to 'follow the yellow brick road.' Look at the signs," Reggie said pointing. That one says 'Follow the red...,' and that one says 'Follow the

21

green....' There has to be one that says 'Follow the yellow...' like in 'follow the yellow brick road!'"

All the campers broke the circle and started running around. A moment later from the other side of the building that held the restrooms they heard someone yell, "Found it!" They all ran to the other side of the building and there it was. A sign next to a pine tree striped in yellow read, "Follow the yellow..."

"This has got to be it," Sally said triumphantly. "Let's circle back up," she called to the group. "Since we are all in this together I think we should vote on this. Raise your hand if you think we should follow the yellow hiking trail." Everybody raised their hand. Reggie smiled with pride as Sally looked at him and said, "Way to go, Reggie."

Before they started down the trail, the kids agreed it would be a good idea to throw all of the boxes and parachutes in the trashcans around the grounds. Those who still had not used the restrooms did so as they all were not sure how long they would be walking the trail.

"I'm glad I wore my tennis shoes," Reggie told Sally as they began walking down the yellow marked trail.

"I hadn't thought about it until you said that," Sally said, "but when the bus showed up at my house I was wearing flip-flops. They told me I couldn't wear flip-flops on the bus and asked me to put on some sneakers. What's going on here?"

"Good question," Reggie answered. "Do you think our parents know they are doing this to us? Is it safe to have a bunch of kids romping about the woods alone?"

"Who knows," Sally answered. "Let's just have fun."

"You're right," Reggie agreed. "This is actually pretty cool. Kind of like a movie, don't you think?"

"It is definitely the craziest thing that has ever happened to me," Sally said laughing.

The group of kids walked for fifteen to twenty minutes through thick woods, open areas, up and down. A girl named Bonnie was leading the pack when the trail split. The yellow rings around the trees could be seen down both paths. "It looks like it is time to make another choice using the riddle," Bonnie announced to the group as they all stopped walking.

Without any direction the campers formed a circle as Sally pulled the note with the riddle out of her back pocket. Some of the kids opened their water bottles and drank. Sweat ran down their faces, and their hair glistened at the temples. With the water bottles closed and everyone paying attention, Sally read the second line of the riddle. "'Take a part a guitar,'" she read slowly. Everyone thought and Sally again read the line slow and loud.

The boy who had earlier said he was good with riddles whose name was Charles said, "I think it is important that it says 'a part' and not apart. To take apart would mean to remove pieces. I think the answer to this riddle is the name of a certain part on a guitar."

"Do you play the guitar?" Sally asked Charles.

"No," he answered. "I don't know anything about them."

"Who here plays the guitar?" Sally asked the group. No one answered. Two girls, obviously friends, were nudging each other. The girl named Olivia did most of the nudging while her friend Mia kept shaking her head "no" as she stared at the ground. From the look on her face, Mia was shy.

When Mia didn't say anything, Olivia ratted her out saying, "Mia plays the guitar. Her mom has made her take lessons since she was seven."

"Why didn't you say anything?" Sally asked.

"She's shy," her friend Olivia answered.

"Oh," Sally said. "It's OK. We need your help, Mia." Sally walked across the circle and stood in front of Mia so she would not feel as though everyone was looking at her. Sally remembered a story she read once where the shy girl in the story wished she was invisible. "What are some different parts of the guitar?"

"Well," Mia began, "a guitar has tuning pegs, a neck, and frets."

"No," Sally frowned. "I don't think any of those work with our riddle. What else?"

Mia thought. "A guitar has strings, a bridge. A bridge!" Mia yelled. "The riddle is telling us to take a bridge!"

Nobody could believe this shy girl had just screamed with such enthusiasm. Mia surprised even herself. She stared again at her feet and the dirt as if something interesting was happening down there.

The campers began to study the two directions in which the trail led. A bridge could not be seen in either direction. As the unofficial leader, Sally suggested, "Why don't the boys check that way," she said pointing to her left "and the girls will check that way," she said pointing to her right. "We will meet back here in five to ten minutes. Don't go too far."

The boys rounded the corner out of sight from the girls. Reggie led the group followed by Charles, Justin, Benjamin, and Josh. A small creek trickled across their path. A large frog could jump over this creek. No need for a bridge. Around the next corner the boys viewed a grassy valley that stretched for what seemed like miles with no bridges to be seen. The boys turned around hoping the girls had found a bridge.

Sally led the girls. Bonnie, Deondra, Olivia, and Mia followed. Within fifty steps the girls began to hear what sounded like gusts of wind. Twenty more steps and it didn't sound like wind anymore, but the distinctive sound of rushing water. The girls ran over a ridge and there it was—a beautiful, enormous, wooden bridge!

"Oh Mia," said Deondra with glee. "You did it girl. You solved the second part of the riddle."

Mia smiled with pride and said, "Let's go back and tell the boys."

"Lead the way," Sally instructed.

Delighted, Mia lead the girls back toward the group of boys. They found them sitting, all staring in their direction with hope. Just before they started back, the girls decided to play a trick on the boys, it was Bonnie's idea. Bonnie said it would be a fun prank if the girls were all frowning and told the boys they did not find a bridge.

As they neared, one of the boys said, "Oh no, they all look sad. Look at their faces. They didn't find a bridge. What are we going to do now?"

Another boy said, "We must have read the riddle wrong."

When the girls were standing in front of the boys Bonnie said, "I hope you guys didn't find a bridge." Bonnie's face still held a deep frown.

"I'm confused," said Reggie. "Why wouldn't you want us to find a bridge?"

All at once the girls said, "Because we did! We did!" They chanted this rehearsed phrase as they danced around and began to laugh in good natured fun.

"You dirty rats!" Reggie said, as all the boys began to laugh along with the girls.

"You really fooled us," Charles said. "I didn't know what we were going to do if you girls didn't find a bridge."

"We better get moving," Sally said. "We still have two more clues we need to figure out."

The bridge stood at least fifty feet above the water. Through the wooden planks that lined the floor, the water below could be seen gushing over rocks and pounding the boulders as it spit a white spray of mist in the air. The brave campers crept across the bridge, concentrating on every step. Sally thought they might have a problem when Benjamin confessed he was afraid of heights and would be unable to cross the bridge. He said he would have to find another way around. Thankfully, Reggie came up with a game to get Benjamin across, and luckily Benjamin felt adventurous enough to play.

"Let's pretend that Benjamin's been hurt," Reggie started. "The hospital is on the other side of the bridge and if we can get him there, he will live. Does anybody have a bandana?" Reggie asked. Deondra and Justin both had bandanas. Reggie took the two bandanas and tied them together. With Sally's help Reggie tied the bandanas around Benjamin's head covering his ears and eyes. Benjamin could still hear the water coursing under the bridge, but it was not as loud and intimidating as before. He could not see at all. Reggie instructed Benjamin to lie on the ground on his back. Two of the kids each grabbed an arm and two more each grabbed a leg. As they lifted Benjamin off the ground Reggie began to make the sound of an ambulance, and the others joined in as well. With the ambulance noises the kids were making and the bandana covering his ears, Benjamin could not hear the sounds of the water at all. As they crossed the bridge, Reggie continued to make siren noises as he watched Benjamin. It was working! At the beginning of the bridge Benjamin smiled with worry. By the middle he laughed with true joy at the game. At the end of the bridge they set him down, pulled the bandana off his face and the kids cheered and danced around him in triumph. Benjamin looked back at the bridge satisfied with his achievement.

After the trail crossed the bridge, the path wound around in what seemed like a circle, bent back and forth, and began a steady climb up the mountain. A network of roots snaked across the path near the top of the crest which also happened to be its steepest point. The campers carefully climbed the roots like rungs on a ladder. The campers topped the mountain and immediately noticed the trail broke into three trails. One of the trails followed the ridge of the mountain. The other two trails dipped into the valley below. One of the trails had an easy slope toward the bottom. The other dropped sharply to the floor of the valley.

Sally pulled the riddle out of her pocket as the campers once again circled up. They all looked to her as their unspoken leader, and she read her note. "'A valley the opposite of life.' Charles?" Sally spoke, looking Charles in the eyes. "Do you have any ideas about this one?"

"Well sure," Charles answered. "This one is easy. The opposite of life is death. The answer to this riddle is Death Valley."

"OK," Sally said agreeing. "Who knows anything about Death Valley? I know it is a place in the United

States, but that is all I remember." Sally waited and when no one responded she asked, "Mia, do you know anything about this one?" Mia shook her head "no." "Somebody here has to," Sally thought and said aloud.

"Death Valley is the lowest point in North America. It is in the Mojave Desert. And that is all I remember." Justin, who had said nothing all day, offered this information.

"We need to take the trail that goes all the way to the valley floor," Charles said. If Death Valley is the lowest elevation in North America, I think the riddle is telling us to take the trail that goes the lowest."

"I agree," Reggie said.

"I do too," Sally agreed. "All of those in favor of taking that trail raise your hand." Everybody raised their hand. "OK. Justin, we would not have figured this one out without you, why don't you lead."

Justin smiled shy and proud and said, "OK." He headed off down the trail and the other campers followed. The path dropped quickly and dangerously toward the valley. Loose rocks licked at the soles of their shoes requiring great concentration and balance from the campers. Justin led with extreme caution, calling out warnings of obstacles ahead as he saw them first. From the sound of his voice, he was not used to speaking to a large group of kids or holding a leadership role. With each command his voice gained a little more strength. At one point about halfway down, Justin stopped the group by holding up his hand and saying, "Hey guys, I think we should stop for a few minutes, and take a drink. I think walking down such a steep slope might be harder than walking up one." Some of the kids agreed as they opened their water bottles and drank. From the distance came the sound of a bark.

"I hope that wasn't a wolf or a coyote," Reggie said.

"Nah," Sally answered. "That was a dog. Sounded like two dogs really."

"Why would two dogs be way out here?" Reggie wondered aloud.

"Maybe they are hiking with their owners," Justin said.

"Makes sense," Sally answered.

"Is everybody ready to go?" Justin asked. The group nodded their heads, put away their bottles, and headed once again carefully down the steep trail.

As the trail leveled off at the valley's floor the group of campers spied a pavilion. A tin roof covered ten or so picnic tables. The pavilion also had two restrooms, a couple of water fountains, and two dogs. Their owners were nowhere to be seen. The two dogs lay there as if they owned the place or were very comfortable there. Reggie thought at first glance they must be lost. As he studied the dogs' frames he decided they were not lost as the two were obviously well fed. Still he wondered, *why are they way out here alone?*

As the group of campers approached the pavilion the dogs eyed them without worry. These dogs were obviously comfortable with and trusting of people. Under the pavilion, some of the boys and girls disappeared into the bathrooms. The dogs fell asleep. One of them even snored.

Reggie and Sally locked eyes. Smiles passed between the two. They both loved this adventure. A break from their semi-boring lives.

"You having fun yet?" Sally asked Reggie.

"Oh yeah," Reggie answered.

"What does the fourth line of the riddle say?" Sally asked Reggie. "Do you remember it by heart?"

"I do," Reggie answered. "It says, 'Hocus Pocus go home.' Where is Charles?"

"He went to the bathroom," Sally answered.

"This one makes no sense," Reggie stated.

"It doesn't," Sally said, leaning in to scratch behind the ears of one of the dogs. As she scratched and petted her eyes lit up. "Reggie," Sally screamed. "Reggie!"

"What?" he asked as he scratched the other dog.

"What is that dog's name?"

"How would I know?"

"Check the collar."

"Oh," Reggie said. He fumbled with the collar, and as he read the name his face lit with recognition of its significance. "It's Pocus."

"This one's name is Hocus," Sally answered.

"Hocus Pocus," they said in unison.

Sally pulled the riddle out of her pocket and read, "'Hocus Pocus go home.'"

"OK," Reggie said. "So we met Hocus and Pocus. They are dogs. Do we tell them to 'go home' as the riddle states?"

"I think that is it," Sally said with excitement. She waited for everybody to come out of the bathroom and gently woke the dogs. Sally looked at the dogs and said, "Hocus, Pocus go home."

The dogs eyed her as they stood. Hocus and Pocus both stretched and turned to walk in the same direction. It surely seemed as if they knew where they were going. The campers followed. Hocus and Pocus, both Labradors, had healthy, shiny coats. The black of Hocus's coat reminded

30

Reggie of midnight. The brilliant blond of Pocus's coat reminded him of his Aunt Rita's hair. His Aunt Rita just turned eighty five and still had beautiful blond hair. Reggie knew nothing of hair color dyes so he just thought she was very lucky to have such beautiful locks.

"Do you think they are leading us to the camp?" Reggie asked Sally as they walked side by side.

"I hope," she responded. "We don't have any more clues."

Hocus and Pocus walked at a steady pace away from the pavilion. The two dogs led the campers through the woods and off the beaten path. The kids had to brush back tree limbs and pull spider webs off of their faces as Hocus and Pocus were short enough to avoid all of these obstacles. Every now and then the dogs would look back to see if they were still being followed. The campers were silent with puzzled looks as they trailed the dogs, still not quite believing what was happening to them. They were following two dogs through the woods!

The campers had been following the dogs for twenty or so minutes when they started to hike up a fairly steep ridge. All of the boys and girls were growing tired and weak. Near the top of the ridge, Hocus and Pocus both let out two barks each and sprinted up and over the crest and out of sight. The campers ran, afraid their guides were leaving them. When they reached the peak they all stopped, stunned at what they saw below. Their faces dropped at the sight. After the amazement their faces transformed into smiles as they imagined themselves down there among the beauty. The beauty that was Camp Timber View.

Chapter 7

As the campers hiked down the ridge toward Camp Timber View they began to hear applause. Near the bottom stood a group of people which included the camp director, counselors, and other campers. The group was well aware of the journey the kids had taken and the obstacles they had overcome. Each of the campers present had been initiated in a similar manner. Each and every face coming down the hill had a happy smile. The joy in Reggie's face turned to puzzlement as he noticed the birdhouses scattered throughout the visible area. Reggie did not have a fear of birds but something about them didn't seem quite right. He forgot about it as his group stopped in front of the cheering crowd.

An older man whom Reggie recognized as the bus driver stepped out of the crowd. He was now wearing a shirt that read, "Camp Director." He was not wearing the glasses or the cape or the other silly items as before. He now looked like a man in charge and not like a character from a cartoon or comic book. He was still tall—you can't easily fake that! And he still had the stark white hair. The camp director raised his hand, and the gesture silenced the crowd.

"I would like to introduce myself and welcome our newest arrivals to Camp Timber View. My name is Gary Slidell; you may call me Mr. Gary." Mr. Gary looked straight at Reggie and Sally's group as he spoke. The other campers had probably already heard this at least once. "This is my first summer here at Camp Timber View, and I hope you can already tell what kind of fun we are going to have this summer by the way in which we brought you here. Sure, we could have just driven the bus straight here.

But that is boring, and that's not the way we're going to spend our summer. Plus, you already got a head start on knowing the people who will be in your living group this summer. That's right," Mr. Gary said, pausing to look around our group, "these are the people you will be spending the majority of your summer with. Along with two counselors, one for the boys and one for the girls, this is what we call your living group."

Two young adults stepped forward out of the crowd and stood next to Mr. Gary. "I would like to introduce Tony and Sissy. They will be your counselors this summer." Both Tony and Sissy nodded their heads and smiled. "Just in case you all ran into any trouble out there on the way here," Mr. Gary said, "Tony and Sissy were following you off in the distance. They are both expert wilderness guides, and I am certain you will all learn a lot from them this summer. And since this is the last group to arrive, I would like all the groups to go to their cabins, get settled, and we will all meet together at the dining hall when the bell rings for supper in an hour and a half."

The boys followed Tony, and the girls followed Sissy in different directions. Reggie and Sally waved to each other without speaking, and before they were out of sight from each other Reggie could hear Sally peppering Sissy with questions. He laughed. The boys did not talk as they followed Tony. Reggie noticed more birdhouses as they made their way to the long row of boys' cabins. "We're going to be in B-8," Tony said, over his shoulder. Tony's hair touched his shoulders. He had dark brown strands of it tucked behind each ear. Tony was not much taller than Reggie's older brother Ronald, but he was muscular and fit. He reminded Reggie of a featherweight boxer. Tony walked with a confidence that was almost a strut.

Cabin B-8 stood ten feet away from the main sidewalk. It had a screened front porch with rocking chairs. The inside of the cabin had four bunk beds. Reggie hoped to get an upper bunk. Cabin B-8 had its own bathroom with one toilet and one shower. Tony immediately claimed these amenities. The kids, he said, could use the bathhouse which was next door. A large curvy hiking stick stood next to Tony's bottom bunk. He told the boys never to wake him by shaking him with their hands. They were to poke him with the hiking stick to wake him. Tony said if you were to wake him by shaking him he might mistake you for an attacker and fight to protect himself. Tony then mumbled something about having nightmares and other dreams that nobody understood or dared to ask.

Reggie got a top bunk. He began setting up his sleeping bag on top of the mattress. His mother wanted to send him sheets, but Reggie said no. He also said no to bringing his Sponge Bob pillow case. As Reggie looked around as the other boys unpacked he realized he was the only boy without a character on his pillow case. He felt sad for a moment to be without it for the entire summer. As he spread his sleeping bag and smoothed out the bumps he felt a strange bump at the bottom of the sleeping bag. Reggie felt it again from the outside of the bag—something was in there. Reggie wondered if it was a dirty sock or something of the like he had left in there from his last camping trip. He reached into the bag and pulled out his Sponge Bob pillow case. It had a rubber band around it and a note from his mom that read, "Just in case you change your mind." Instead of signing the note his mom

34

drew a heart. With the top bunk came a window sill. Reggie set a little picture of his mom and dad in the sill and smiled.

Sally's cabin was G-7. It was much the same as Reggie's other than the fact that the porches were switched. Sally's cabin had a back porch instead of a front porch. Sissy also took a bottom bunk and would not let the girls use the bathroom in the cabin. As soon as Sally saw Sissy's living space she thought she might be a hippy. Silk scarves and ribbons draped down from above Sissy's bed. Sally saw peace signs and posters with words like flower power and Woodstock. Sally recalled Woodstock being a three-day music festival in the late 1960's. Some of her Dad's favorite bands and musicians had played there before *he* was even born. She sat with him one afternoon as he watched something about it on the History Channel. Maybe she would understand it all when she was older she thought.

Sally chose a bottom bunk. She brought sheets. Sally didn't mind sleeping in a sleeping bag from time to time in the tree house or at a sleepover, but an entire summer in a sleeping bag would be too much. She did not have any characters on her sheets, pillow case, or comforter, but she did bring her stuffed pink cat, Pinky. As the other girls saw Sally set her stuffed animal on her pillow they too brought theirs out of hiding. Sissy put on some music while the girls continued to unpack. Sally asked her who it was and learned it was Janis Joplin. Sissy lay on her bed and sang along.

Chapter 8

At six o'clock the bell hanging over the dining hall rang. This, of course, signaled it was time for dinner. Reggie wondered what the food would be like. He wasn't very picky, but he also wouldn't eat just anything. After the long hike though, his hunger was telling him to eat whatever he could get his hands on.

From the outside, the dining hall looked as though it was constructed entirely out of stone. An enormous porch jutted out from the rectangular structure which stood one story above a recreation room and the camp store. Two stone stairways allowed campers to climb up to the porch from opposite directions. One stairway faced the girls' cabins, and the other faced the boys'. Tony led his group up the stairs almost at the same time as Sissy led her girls up the mammoth rock stairs. The two groups spied each other, and they met toward the middle. The campers sat down on the stone benches, and Tony and Sissy spoke quietly with one another. Reggie raised his eyebrows at Sally who smiled back. Reggie didn't want to sit next to Sally as one of the boys had already asked him if she was his girlfriend. Reggie told him he was too young to have a girlfriend and that she was just his neighbor and good friend. Sally had received the same questions from the girls. Both too tired to answer any more of those questions today, they sat apart from one another.

Sissy stood in front of the group and addressed them. "Alright team," she began. "Every night before we go into dinner we will meet on the front dining hall porch with the rest of the camp and have roll call. Let me tell you what roll call is." Sissy paused to collect her thoughts. "Every night the camp director will give us a question or an idea or a theme. When they call our group number, which is group number eleven, we have to all answer together, shouting out our response. Tonight when we do roll call we have to shout out our group's name. So, instead of being called living group number eleven, we need to tell them what to call us from now on. Does anybody have any ideas?"

No one said a thing. After a few moments of silence, Tony said, "How about the Nerds?"

"No!" all the campers responded.

More silence went by. "How about the Dorky Monkeys?" Tony put forth.

"No!" the campers said again.

"Well," Tony said, "if you don't like any of my suggestions, you better come up with one as a group.

The boys talked with the boys, and the girls talked with the girls. Sally, of course led the discussion in the group of girls. The boys, without leadership threw out random ideas.

Here were the ideas for the living group name: Banana Splits, Fried Monsters, Kung Fu Ghosts, Giant Biscuits, Super Frogs, Noodle Juice, McParty Punch, Science Machines, Big Lucky Dogs, and Fire Runts.

Tony and Sissy didn't know what to say to these ideas. Finally Sissy said, "Those are all very creative." She paused, thinking carefully what to say next in hopes she would not hurt their feelings. "I think for today one of those names would be very funny, but what about next week and the week after that. Do you want to be the Fried Monsters every day for the next eight weeks?"

Sally's mind searched and rambled through all of its creative places. As she thought, she saw Reggie's lips moving, but he was not saying anything. Reggie did this when he wanted to say something but wouldn't for one reason or another. At times he could be unsure of himself and shy.

"I can tell Reggie has an idea," Sally blurted out. Reggie shot her a look. It was not a nice look. "I'm sorry, Reggie," Sally said, "but I know you and I can tell you have a good idea."

"What's your idea, Reggie?" Tony asked. "It can't be worse than Noodle Juice!"

Reggie laughed. "Well," Reggie began, "I was thinking that since there are twelve of us, ten kids and two counselors, we could have the number twelve in our name. As I was thinking about that I felt a little thirsty, and my favorite drink is 7UP. So, I thought we could be 12UP." Reggie hung his head unsure of himself again.

"That's awesome, Reggie," Sissy said.

"I really like that," Tony agreed.

"Me too," said Sally. "I knew he had a good idea."

The other kids were nodding their heads yes and agreeing out loud when Sissy called for a vote. "All those in favor of 12UP raise your hand." Everybody raised one of their hands. "It is unanimous," Sissy said. "12UP it is." Reggie smiled as Sissy gave him a wink. Tony patted him on the back as Reggie gave Sally a look that told her she was forgiven for calling him out in such a way.

A few minutes later roll call began. There were seventeen living groups. The camp director, Mr. Gary stood on the stone bench that wrapped around the porch and called the living group numbers. Reggie's stomach growled, and he thought it would take forever to get through seventeen groups. To his surprise and his stomach's happiness, it went pretty fast. Before Reggie knew it, Mr. Gary called, "Living group number ten."

Living group number ten huddled and quietly counted to three before calling out, "Crunchy Kids!"

People laughed and the director waited for quiet before calling, "Living group number eleven."

"OK," Sissy said as the group huddled up. "When I say three, let's yell it as loud as we can. One, two, three."

"12UP," they yelled. Their voices filled the porch with power, and they all sat back down happy with their new name.

"Living group number twelve," Mr. Gary continued.

"Hot, Hot, Hot," they shouted.

"Living group number thirteen."

"The Flip-Flop Bums."

Mr. Gary wrote down every groups' name on a chalkboard that hung behind him. Reggie's church had a few chalkboards in the Sunday school rooms but his school had only whiteboards because some students were allergic to the chalk. After he finished writing living group number seventeen's new name on the board he explained there were two doors to enter the dining hall. He made it clear that a new group would go first each day.

"Tonight," Mr. Gary said, "we will start with Muddy Morning at door number one and 12UP at door number two."

Reggie could not have been happier. He was just about to eat his shirt he was so hungry. Reggie walked in the door, looked at the serving line, and immediately lost his appetite.

Chapter 9

Reggie had never really had a crush before. He was eleven years old for crying out loud. He thought some girls at school were pretty, but that was about it. A lot of girls thought he was cute. Reggie had black curly hair and blue eyes. He was of an average height for his age. Most girls liked him because he was a nice boy, and if that didn't do it for them, his two dimples did.

At the end of the serving line, filling plastic cups with ice, stood Cynthia. Reggie would later discover she was from Acapulco, Mexico. Her parents ran the dining hall and she and her fourteen year old brother Oscar helped her parents during the summer. Cynthia was twelve. On this particular evening she wore a red bandana tied loosely around her head. Her curly black hair flowed out of the bandana and over her shoulders. Some of it spilled down her back. Her eyes were as dark as midnight. Her long eyelashes blinked Reggie's way, and he felt as if he was going to be sick. Reggie had never felt this way before. He wanted to jump in the air, scream at the top of his lungs, and lie down to die.

The next few minutes were a mass of confusion. Reggie went through the serving line and got two fish sticks and a small box of Captain Crunch. He had no idea how this had happened. As he sat down at a table he held in his hand dreamily a plastic cup filled with ice.

"She's not *that* pretty," Sally said, sitting across the table from Reggie.

"What?" Reggie asked, snapping out of a daydream.

"I said, she is not that pretty."

"She is," Reggie replied. "Have you ever felt like this?" Reggie asked.

"Of course I have," Sally answered. "Do you remember Craig Minters?"

"Yeah."

"I think I felt the same way about him as you do about the girl in the serving line."

"What did you do about it?" Reggie asked.

"Nothing," Sally answered.

"Didn't his family move to Texas?" Reggie asked.

"Yep, and I never saw him again."

"I'm sorry," Reggie said.

"You get over it," Sally assured.

"I'll never get over her."

"Shut up and eat your fish sticks and Captain Crunch."

After dinner, all of the campers gathered around a giant campfire for an evening of storytelling. Each living group told of their riddle and how they made their way to the camp. Much of the telling was enhanced by the counselors who had been watching in the distance of the woods. When it came time for 12UP to speak, Sally and Sissy did most of the talking. Tony added a few funny observations, and Reggie only remembered Cynthia.

The next morning when the camp bell rang to wake everyone, Tony was still snoring. Reggie had been awake in his sleeping bag for ten or so minutes thinking and wondering about the day ahead. The other boys were sound asleep when it rang and slow to roll out of bed and wake up. Knowing they needed their leader awake, Reggie jumped off his bunk and slowly crept up to Tony's bunk.

The crooked hiking stick leaned against his bunk. With his nerves in a knot, Reggie picked up the hiking stick. He held it at an angle, pointing it at Tony's ribcage—breathed in—and finally poked.

As if Tony's arm was a striking snake it lashed out and grabbed the end of the hiking stick. Thankfully he did not pull Reggie to him as there was no telling what danger Reggie would have been in if he did and Reggie landed on top of him. Instead, after Tony grabbed the stick he suddenly sat up in bed with a fright and thrust the stick away from his body. The force luckily did not jab the hiking stick into Reggie's own body, but it did knock him off balance enough to send him tumbling to the floor.

The noise woke the entire room, and Reggie remained motionless on the floor staring wide-eyed at Tony.

"Oh my goodness," Tony apologized. "Are you alright?"

"I'm fine," Reggie answered. "You just spooked me."

"I forgot to tell you to poke me in the feet with the hiking stick and not anywhere near my hands."

"That information would have been very helpful," Reggie said with a smile breaking across his face. "I think tomorrow it will be somebody else's turn."

At breakfast, Reggie did not see Cynthia. Sally saw him looking for her but she did not say anything about it. Tony asked Reggie to tell the other campers in their living group about how he woke him up, but Reggie did not feel up to speaking to the group and shook his head no. Tony told the story and received a lot of laughs. Reggie laughed as well as it was kind of funny now that it was in the past.

After breakfast, Tony and Sissy gave the group a tour of the camp grounds. They started the tour on the bottom floor of the dining hall which held a recreation room and the camp store. The recreation room was called the Rec and had pool tables, foosball, ping pong, air hockey, checkers tables, and stacks of other board games. Comfortable couches and beanbags were scattered throughout the room. Reggie noticed one of the birdhouses high in one of the corners. The camp store did not have too many offerings. A sign above the cash register read "Tina's Cantina." Sally wondered if there really was a Tina or if the camp was just trying to come up with a name that rhymed. The store sold drinks, ice-cream, candy, and camp t-shirts. You could also buy stamps and time on an ancient telephone. Another sign read, "5 minutes—1 Dollar $$."

"Now we are going to show you the pool where we will go swimming and the lake where we will teach canoeing," Sissy announced.

As they walked toward the pool Reggie noticed a few more of the strange birdhouses. He quietly asked Sally, "Are you noticing all of these birdhouses?"

"I guess they do seem to have a lot of them," she answered.

"Did you notice the one in the Rec? Do the birds come inside at this camp?"

"I didn't see that one," Sally said.

"Don't you think that is a little weird?" Reggie asked.

"I guess so. I wouldn't get all worked up about it though."

"I'm not getting worked up. I just think it is weird that there are so many of them. I've only seen one bird and who knows how many birdhouses."

"That is a very lucky bird," Sally joked.

"I bet if we look at lunch, we will find one in the dining hall."

"You're nuts," Sally said.

"Then let's make a bet," Reggie said.

"Did you already see one in there?" Sally asked. "If you did then it is not a fair bet."

"I swear I didn't," Reggie answered.

"Pinky swear," Sally said, holding out her pinky.

"Pinky swear," Reggie said, latching his pinky with hers.

The size of the pool surprised all of the kids. In almost every pool Reggie had swam in he could swim from one end to the other under water without taking a breath. He estimated it would take three or four breaths to swim across this one. Also, in most of the pools where he swam there were no diving boards. When Reggie asked why, his dad said something about insurance and people suing other people, all of which he did not understand. This enormous pool had two diving boards—a low board and a high dive. It also had a slide that looked like a curly french-fry. All the campers wanted to swim immediately, but the tour was not over.

The lake was not quite as exciting as the pool. It was a small lake. There were canoes, paddles, and a dock. Sally could not help but think of snakes.

"Are there snakes in there?" she asked.

Tony and Sissy looked at each other and some sort of non-verbal communication passed between the two of them. "I have never seen one," Sissy finally said.

"I haven't either," Tony said. He didn't sound very sincere.

"Even if there are," Sissy added, "you will be in a boat."

"So," Sally said, "you are not going to tip our boat over to teach us how to save a capsized boat or anything like that?" she asked.

The look passed between Tony and Sissy again. It was a look that Sally did not like very much. "We don't have any plans to do that at this point," Tony answered.

"At this point?" Sally asked.

"None at this point," Tony answered. Changing the subject he said, "Let's go see the gym and the ball fields."

The gym had basketball goals, volleyball nets, indoor soccer goals, baskets full of footballs, and a large stage. Reggie pointed out two birdhouses to Sally who was now becoming a little concerned about them. The ball field sat in the center of the camp. Some of the boys' cabins sat along the first base side. The camp clinic was just beyond right-center field. Reggie could see a nurse through a large window. The window didn't seem far enough away from home plate to Reggie.

"How many times have those windows been smashed out?" Reggie asked the counselors.

"Never," Tony answered. "Counselors are not allowed to bat with two hands. We have to swing the bat with just one. It is a safety thing. And no kid can hit that far," Tony said with confidence.

"I can," Reggie said.

"Sure you can," Tony said, as he playfully tossed Reggie's curly hair around in his fingers.

"Who wants to see the waterfall?" Sissy asked. All the kids nodded their heads in agreement. "We don't have a lot of hard and fast rules around here," Sissy said, turning serious. "But here are two. You may never, ever swim at the bottom of the falls without a counselor. And at the top of the falls, nobody, even a counselor may cross the fence. Although it is very beautiful, it is also very dangerous. Are we all very clear about this?" The campers all nodded their heads. "If you are caught breaking either of these two rules, you will be sent home. I would hate to see that happen." Sissy eyed all of the campers with a grave expression. When she had made eye contact with all of them her dreary looked disappeared and was replaced with a smile. "Let's go see it," she said.

12UP walked along toward the falls. They were quiet as all eyes took note of the surroundings. As the eyes drank, all eyes saw it—somehow, a giant barn-like structure stood out of the side of a baby mountain. Sissy said, "We square-dance there." All of the campers exchanged looks.

Camp Timber View called the falls the Chimney Creek Falls. They did look like a giant and very wide chimney. As 12UP walked toward the falls they could hear them well before they could see them. The crushing of water against water and rock was a powerful sound. They all knew it was big before it came into sight. As the group rounded a corner and crested a hill they all at once stopped and stared. Chimney Creek Falls was magnificent, spectacular, awesome, and even a little bit unbelievable. A paradise for water.

Reggie and Sally had both seen a number of waterfalls, but this was the widest falls either of them remembered seeing. The water crashed into a pool below and Sally said, "I can see why you wouldn't want us to swim under there."

"Pulls you right under," Sissy said.

"That water is stronger than any man," Tony said thoughtfully.

"Appreciate it at a distance," Sissy added.

Just then the giant sound of a deep and heavy bell filled the air.

"Lunch," said Reggie with a smile, thinking of Cynthia.

"One more thing before we go and eat," Tony said. "Just beyond the top of the falls is the beginning of our trails. We have three. One goes straight up the mountain to the ropes course. I will tell you all more about that later. The second travels along the creek on the opposite side of the main camp. It leads to the camping field. And the third is a secret." With that said, Tony turned and said, "Let's go get some grub."

Chapter 10

Upon entering the dining hall, Reggie noticed Cynthia dressing the salads, and he assumed she was working the salad bar for lunch. Reggie didn't like salad a whole lot but decided to give it another try. As he took a plate from the stack at the beginning of the bar he felt his stomach wrench into knots. Goosebumps tickled his back. The sensation caused him to flinch, and his head bobbed unnaturally.

"Are you alright?" Cynthia asked. She smiled.

"I..." Reggie tried. He felt like an idiot. "Yes, I'm fine." Reggie sighed. "Just a chill, I think."

"Enjoy your lunch," Cynthia said.

"Me will," Reggie answered.

When he sat down next to Sally she was laughing and said, "Me will?"

"I meant, I will," Reggie snapped.

"You didn't get a drink," Sally noticed. "I'm going to get some lemonade. Do you want me to get you some too?"

"Please."

"OK, me will," Sally said, walking away laughing with a good natured chuckle.

On her return, Sally set the glass of lemonade in front of him and said, "So, you are no Prince Charming."

"Can we just drop it?" Reggie pleaded.

"Sure, I'm sorry. I've just never seen you all torn up about a girl."

"I said to drop it."

"Dropped," Sally said, making a motion with both hands like she was dropping something. "You won the bet," she said changing the subject.

"What bet?" Reggie asked.

"I see two birdhouses," Sally said, pointing with her eyes.

"Oh my goodness," Reggie said, "what is going on with those?"

"I will admit it is a bit fishy," Sally answered.

By this point all of the other kids in their group had sat down and were curiously listening to their conversation.

"What are you two talking about?" Charles asked.

Reggie and Sally exchanged a secretive glance, and they each nodded in unison.

"The birdhouses everywhere," Sally said. "Have you noticed them?"

Charles shook his head no. Benjamin said, "I have seen a few and even one in the gym. I thought it was kind of weird."

"I was wondering why there were two of them in here," Deondra said. "I saw you two looking at them," she said looking at Reggie and Sally.

"Why doesn't somebody just ask about them?" Bonnie suggested.

"I will," Josh offered.

"OK," Sally said. "When Tony and Sissy sit down, you ask. Don't ask right away though. Make it seem like something that you just thought of that isn't very important."

The counselors were always last to sit down as it was their job to supervise and help the campers as they went through the lines. After Tony and Sissy sat down, Josh waited through a few minutes of light conversation before pretending to notice one of the birdhouses in a corner of the dining hall.

"Why in the world is there a birdhouse in the dining hall?" Josh asked. He was a good actor. If Reggie had not known he had already seen it, he would have believed Josh was seeing it for the first time.

Tony and Sissy once again exchanged the glance that Sally did not like.

"Oh," Tony said. "Funny story. This camp has not always been named Camp Timber View. This is actually its first year *as* Camp Timber View. For the last thirty-six years it had been Camp Birdsong. The previous directors and counselors liked the bird theme and hung birdhouses everywhere, including a lot of indoor places."

"Well, that explains that," Josh said.

Chapter 11

12UP signed up for the first campout of the summer. Both Tony and Sissy loved spending the night out under the stars. There were no tents at a Camp Timber View campout. After lunch the group split to pack their backpacks which came in the trunk of goodies delivered to their homes. The campers were instructed to pack their sleeping bags, one change of clothes, flashlights, water bottles, and even their cameras.

As they packed, Reggie turned to Tony and asked, "Are we bringing food?"

"There is an old logging road that can get out there from the opposite direction and the food supplies will be delivered after we get there. We will be making hobo dinners and smores."

"What is a hobo dinner?" Justin asked.

"You will have to wait and see," Tony answered, with a devious grin. "Has anybody met Mr. George yet?" The boys shook their heads no. "He is the one who will be delivering the food supplies. You are in for a real treat with this guy. He is Mr. Gary's father. He'll probably tell you all a ghost story if you want him to."

The boys met the girls at the top of the falls. They crossed the bridge across the water and began walking the trail that led to the campground. Trees created a canopy above the trail, and the light filtering through falling on the trail reminded Reggie of golden sunflowers and a painting he remembered by Vincent Van Gogh. The trail followed the creek for a while and it was fairly flat and an easy hike. As they walked this part Sissy took the lead and started a game. She would introduce a category like soft drinks and then she would name one. Everybody behind her had to say one in line order. If you took too long to say one or could not think of one you had to go to the back of the line. Some of the categories were countries, bands, candies, instruments, things from the circus, and sports teams. When Sissy ran out of ideas, Tony took the lead. Reggie only had to go to the back of the line one time. Sally never did; she had always been a quick thinker. Mia spent a lot of time at the back—she was back to being shy again. Tony said after a few days the campers would not be able to shut her up. He said he had seen her type before.

The group stopped playing the game as the trail reached a rather overgrown stretch. Sissy explained that the trail had not been hiked in close to a year, so plants had time to grow and reach their limbs and leaves across the trail and up from its path. She said after a few weeks it would look like a trail again after hundreds of footsteps tromped through. Sissy also said the campers were expected to join a service club for the summer, and one of the clubs performed trail maintenance. Some of the other places to do your community service were the craft shack, cleaning and passing out supplies. One could work at the gym and ball field keeping track of equipment and tidying up. A drama club would work on a play for the summer to perform near the end of camp. The Rec needed help making sure all of the pieces were put back in the game boxes. The camp post office used campers to sort and deliver mail to boxes out front of the cabins after it was delivered to the camp. And the final place one could sign up for community service was the dining hall. When Reggie heard this his eyes lit up, and Sally turned around and caught his eye and she winked which made him smile and blush.

When they stopped for a quick water break, Sally sat down next to Reggie. "Now," she began, with a false curiosity, "where are you thinking of signing up for your community service?" Reggie rolled his eyes at her. "Let me guess," she teased. "The mailroom?" Reggie shook his head no. "The trail thing, I know you love wandering around in the woods." Reggie shook his head no again. "Are you possibly going to work in the dining hall with the world's most beautiful girl—Cynthia?"

Reggie smiled and said, "I think me will." Sally rolled on the ground laughing at his comeback.

The camping field was not too far, and they reached it in less than an hour. And it was a field as advertised—a strange, strange sight to be seen right out in the middle of the woods. There were at least two football fields of open area without a single tree. The area was almost a perfect rectangle filled with green grass that had just been obviously cut. Reggie wondered how they had brought the lawn mower up here and then remembered the old logging road that Tony had talked about. Sally looked around and saw the campfire pit and a stack of wood and wondered about the bathrooms.

"Where are the bathrooms?" she asked Sissy.

"Great question," Sissy answered. "Everybody listen up," she said. "Since we are in the woods, we of course do not have any bathrooms. When you need to go to the bathroom, the girls will walk that way," she said pointing in one direction, "and the boys will walk that way," she said pointing in the other. "Walk far enough from camp that you cannot be seen, and take care of your business."

All of a sudden everybody's ears perked up as they heard the motor of an automobile approaching. They also heard two barks. It was Mr. George coming up the old logging road with the food supplies. Hocus and Pocus were in the back, tongues wagging as they hung off each side of the truck peering forward. The truck was an ancient red Chevrolet. He parked it at the edge of the tree line and Hocus and Pocus jumped out and ran toward the group. Mr. George slowly opened the door of the truck and lit an enormous cigar. Once satisfied the cigar was burning the way he liked, he proceeded to limp into camp.

"I thought nobody was allowed to smoke at Camp Timber View," Sally said.

"Mr. George does not follow that rule," Tony said. "He is a war veteran and claims he has earned the right to do as he pleases. I am sure he will tell you all about it in just a minute." Tony smiled a knowing smile.

As Mr. George neared, all of the campers watched him hobble. He wore blue faded overalls with a red shirt underneath. He wore a dark green bandana around his neck like a necklace. His boots looked brand new and recently shined. A curly mess of gray and white hair sat atop his head. He puffed the cigar to keep it burning, and smoke billowed around his head.

"What in the world are all of you just standing around for?" Mr. George asked. "Unload the truck!" He puffed the giant cigar, and the stink of it had Reggie thinking of burning honey. Reggie hurried off to help unload the truck. Hocus and Pocus decided to follow.

When they returned, Mr. George told them where to put all of the supplies. Mr. George sat down, and all of the campers had their eyes fixed on him. They were not sure if they should be frightened of him or amused. Hocus and Pocus obviously felt comfortable with him as they both lay by him, one on each side.

Tony broke the mood by announcing, "We need to collect wood! Only dead wood," he instructed. "Get three handfuls each!"

When they were out of earshot Sally asked, "What is up with that guy?"

"I think he will be alright," Reggie answered. "He's just old. Do you remember my great uncle Douglas? He reminds me of him."

"How could I ever forget him," Sally said with a laugh. "He always called me silly instead of Sally and he thought he was so clever. I'll never forget the day we were standing in your driveway before your parents had it paved, and it was still dirt." Reggie laughed picturing in his mind the story she was recalling. "He got into his car, which had the window rolled down and for some reason you asked him to lay a wheel."

"I was just making a joke," Reggie said trying to defend himself.

"Well, he took you seriously and almost flipped the car over. The car fishtailed sideways, and the wheels shot dirt in the open window and all over your parents' bedspread." Reggie bent over laughing. "And that wasn't the worst of it. He lost control of the car and ran over your mailbox."

"I think Mom was madder about the bedspread," Reggie said.

When they returned to camp with their third load of wood, Reggie and Sally dropped their loads onto the mammoth pile. Sissy asked the campers to gather around for a demonstration on how to start a fire. Sissy had them separate the wood they had gathered into four piles. The four piles were: 1) Smaller than a pinkie finger 2) About the size of a pencil 3) Nearly the size of your stretched out arm 4) Everything else.

When the campers finished all of the sorting, Sissy asked them all to take a seat around the fire pit. Tony was in the woods looking for big pieces that would burn long into the night. With the campers gathered around the fire pit, Sissy showed them how she looked for the thinnest pieces from her smaller than a pinkie stack first. She liked to find one piece that looked like a capital letter Y first and another straight piece that would lie propped in the crook of the Y. With these two pieces as her beginning point she created a teeny tiny teepee. The campers watched with anticipation and amazement.

"How is that going to make a fire?" Justin asked. "That's so small. Why don't you just pour some gas on it or something?"

Sissy smiled at him. "We don't have any gas, Justin."

"Mr. George could have brought some," he answered.

"Adding gas to a fire is dangerous. Plus, this is a very good skill to know. Get me one handful of pine straw and one handful of dried leaves," Sissy instructed Justin.

Justin did as she asked. "Now," Sissy said. "Insert one piece of pine straw at a time in between our kindling. Kindling is the correct term for this wood."

"You mean it is not called wood smaller than a pinkie finger?" Deondra asked, teasing.

"No. Don't you think that would have been a better name?" The kids laughed, and some of them nodded affirmatively.

"This is kind of like a game," Justin announced to the group as he poked pieces of pine straw through the tiny openings. He smiled.

When he finished, Sissy said, "Now, take the dried leaves and crush them." Justin did as asked. "Sprinkle them over our creation." He did.

"Now," Sissy said. "If we did this right it should only take one match to cook our supper and keep us warm. She handed the book of matches to Justin and said, "Please do the honors."

"Really?" he asked.

"Really," Sissy answered.

Justin struck the match and held it against a strand of pine straw at the base of the fire. After a moment the piece of pine straw ignited and Justin dropped the match and stood back, watching. The tiny piece of pine straw lit another piece of pine straw which lit another piece and before long all of the straws were ablaze. The flames curling up through the tiny sticks caught the dried leaves above on fire, and the tiny sticks lit a moment later.

"Now," Sissy said, breaking the trance of the campers staring into the fire. "At this point you have to be ready with pile number two—about the size of a pencil. Carefully lay sticks of this size one at a time around the perimeter of your fire. The fire will quickly burn what you have given it, and the fire will need more fuel. If you give it something too big at this point, it will not be ready, and it will choke and die out. Mia," she called, "come do this for us."

Mia hopped up and did just as asked. She carefully laid sticks across the fire, and it seemed as soon as Mia laid them across the flames they were devoured. Sissy told the group that since the weather had been so dry the past few weeks and all of their wood was very dry the fire would burn through it very fast. Sissy told them that sometimes when the wood was a little damp they might have to blow into the fire to provide it oxygen. Not tonight though she said. Mia quickly piled all of the sticks in the second pile on the fire as it was now roaring.

Sissy called Olivia to put the next size pieces on the fire. As she did the light slowly started to fade from the sky, and the orange of the fire seemed to intensify. Mr. George lit his cigar, again and the sweet burnt honey smell drifted around the camp. Tony decided to call it quits as he had found enough wood to start a wood pile.

"And that is how you make a fire," Sissy said to the group but winking at Justin. She looked at Tony and said, "Why don't you teach them how to make a hobo dinner."

"I would love to," Tony answered. "Let's sit at the picnic tables for this," Tony said, directing the kids to the tables under the pavilion. He flicked a switch, and light poured down on the tables. "Thank goodness for technology," he said. "Now, take a large piece of foil." Sissy passed the boxes of foil to each table, and the campers began to tear large sections from the roll. "Now," Tony continued, "Mr. George and Sissy will give you the vegetables, and it is your job to cut them up."

"Who is going to give us the knives?" Sally asked aloud.

Tony smiled as if he had been waiting for such a question. "You already have them," Tony answered.

"What?" Sally asked. "No we don't."

"You do," Tony answered. "Your teeth."

"My what?" Deondra asked, moving her head side to side and pointing her finger at her own mouth.

"Yep," Tony answered, "your mouth. Take bites and spit it in your tin foil. The spit will cook right off and it's your spit anyway—it's going to be in your mouth eventually. What does it matter if it is in your mouth, out of your mouth, and back in again? Watch!" he instructed.

Tony took a medium sized carrot from Mr. George and bit and pushed and bit and pushed until the entire carrot was in his mouth in bite-size pieces. He grabbed his piece of foil and spit his mouthful of carrot into the center. "Nothing to it," he said. "Please give me a potato, Mr. George. Now, the raw potato taste may take a few bites to get used to, but it's not too bad."

Hesitantly, the campers began to do as asked. When Sissy pulled out the ground beef, Deondra said, "Oh no! I'll do a lot of things you might ask me, but I am not chewing up that raw meat!"

Sissy, Tony, and Mr. George guffawed. Sissy told the kids that she would be the one pulling apart the ground beef with her hands and putting it in each hobo dinner. After she did this and all the vegetables were cut up, Tony taught them how to fold the aluminum foil into a tight little package. He said they had to wait until the fire burned down to coals to put them on the fire, and in the meantime they could all, excluding Mr. George, get one more handful of wood.

When they returned from the woods they found Mr. George's cigar burning on the ground by the chair he had been sitting in when they left. Oddly, his shiny boots, his truck keys, and his dark green bandana lay next to the cigar. Mr. George had disappeared.

Chapter 12

Hocus and Pocus barked and howled like mad wolves. The campers scrambled. Tony and Sissy watched. As the campers looked to Sissy and Tony for leadership, Tony walked toward them and tripped. On the ground he grabbed his knee and winced in what looked like tremendous pain.

"Oh Sissy," he said. "It's the same knee I had surgery on two months ago. You have to take me to the infirmary in the truck now!"

"What?" Sally asked. "You are leaving? You are leaving us with an old man who has disappeared in the woods? This isn't right!"

"He needs medical attention, Sally," Sissy responded. "Hocus and Pocus are excellent tracking dogs. Sometimes Mr. George gets confused and wanders off. He won't be far. Get your flashlights out of your backpack, let Hocus and Pocus smell his bandana and give them the command to track."

"Is this a joke?" Josh asked.

"No," Tony said through clinched teeth. "Mr. George probably forgot to take his medication tonight. He's probably right over the ridge there," he said pointing at the sky. "I'll tell Mr. Gary when we get back to camp what is happening, and we will bring back his medication. You all get Mr. George, and we will get his meds."

Sissy told Tony to sit still as she grabbed Mr. George's keys and sprinted toward the old red Chevy. She cranked the truck and pulled it up right next to where he lay on the ground, still clutching at his knee. Sissy put the truck in park and ran around the front of the truck. She opened the passenger door and helped Tony into his seat.

Sissy slammed the door shut and ran around the front of the truck again and hopped back into her seat. She slammed her door shut with urgency. "Go find Mr. George," she called out of the open window. "I will meet you back here in one hour." With this said, she sped off down the old logging road and out of sight.

The campers stood staring at one another in disbelief. A man had mysteriously disappeared and their adult leaders had abandoned them. They could not believe this. Silence hung in the air as the sound of the truck faded. The fire cracked and popped. Hocus and Pocus whimpered.

Reggie looked at Sally. For once in her life she was speechless. He looked around at the other campers. Their faces were blank. "We have to do something!" Reggie pronounced. "We have to find Mr. George. Everybody get your flashlight." Reggie could not believe he was giving out commands. His first command was so weak that nobody moved. "Get your flashlights!" he bellowed, with his next command. "We don't have any time to waste. There is an old man lost in the woods who is off his medication." The campers moved with Reggie's urgency. They scurried to their packs and retrieved their flashlights. The sun and all of its light had completely faded.

Reggie pointed to Sally who was starting to come around and said, "Get Mr. George's bandana." Sally ran over to the spot where he had been sitting and picked up his bandana. "Let Hocus and Pocus smell it," Reggie instructed. Sally called the dogs and held the bandana down to their noses. They sniffed and sniffed until Reggie called their names.

"Hocus," Reggie said loudly, "Pocus," he uttered with the same determination. "Track."

The dogs took off, bounding over all obstacles in their way to get to the scent. The kids followed. Thank God Sissy and Tony had just curiously put the two dogs on leashes. Reggie held one and Sally the other as they were pulled through the woods.

The campers ran after the dogs and when the dogs slowed, the campers in turn slowed their pace. When the dogs lost the scent, stopped and barked, nobody could believe what they saw. Hocus and Pocus both lay down at the sight. The kids shined their flashlights on the center of the lake. Mr. George was sitting in the center of the lake in a rocking chair.

The next morning they woke up at the campground in sleeping bags on a tarp in the open air. The campers' and counselors' sleeping bags glistened, wet with dew. The campers' minds were still foggy with the previous night's events. Tony, Sissy, and Mr. Gary had arrived at the lake just after their discovery. With a boat that happened to be tied to a nearby tree, they retrieved Mr. George. Back at the campsite, Tony pulled the hobo dinners off the fire, and they were incredibly well done. Some of the vegetables were nearly black, and the ground beef crunched in their mouths. As they were all exhausted and bewildered from the adventure, they decided as a group to skip the smores and save them for another campout.

Sally rarely had nothing to say. On the hike back to camp, she as well as the other campers was silent. Only the sounds of boots and birds and wind filled the air. As they neared camp, the sounds of a small city began to fill the air. As the campers descended the final slope into camp, Sissy announced that the group would have two hours of free time after breakfast. They could take showers, visit the Rec or Tina's Cantina, go swimming—it didn't matter as long as they stayed within the limits of the camp. Sissy also explained they would have an additional hour and a half of free time before dinner. During one of these times they were expected to contact and make arrangements with the leaders of the different service groups. Sissy said there was a list posted in the Rec of who to contact.

Reggie avoided Cynthia during breakfast as he had not showered or brushed his hair. Immediately after breakfast he ran to cabin B-8, grabbed his bathroom bag and towel and headed for the showers. He didn't have to tell Sally where he was going or what he was doing, she knew.

Showered and dressed, Reggie took extra care brushing his hair. He could feel his pulse racing as his heart beat against his chest. He wasn't even going to look at the list in the Rec, he decided just to go straight to the dining hall. As he ascended the dining hall stairs Reggie slowed to catch his breath and to compose himself. He took one final breath and pulled on the dining hall door. Locked.

Undeterred, Reggie knew there must be a back door for deliveries and taking out the trash. As he crept around the side of the building and rounded toward the back of the dining hall he spotted an old green and rusted dumpster. A sidewalk led from the dumpster to a loading dock. At the back of the loading dock stood an open door into the dining hall. Bingo!

Reggie walked up a narrow stone stairway and tripped over a hose at the top. After catching his fall he steadied himself and peered in the open doorway. Reggie saw a cloud of steam and two pair of feet. Steam poured

63

out of the dishwashing machine. Reggie could not tell to whom the feet belonged.

Instead of intruding, Reggie called, "Hello?... Hello?"

A man suddenly came walking out of the steam and into focus. He had the same color skin as Cynthia, and Reggie surmised that the man must have been her father. "Campers aren't allowed back here," he said. "Get out."

His stern voice almost had Reggie running for the door but he stood his ground. "I am here about the job," Reggie mustered.

"I'm not hiring," the man grumbled. "And anyway, you are too young."

Not knowing what to say to this Reggie stood there flustered. Luckily he was saved by a woman who had overheard their conversation.

"Carlos," she said, with a sweet voice, "he is a camper here for the service project."

"Of course," the man said. He nodded at Reggie and disappeared.

"I am Mrs. Vargas," the lady with the sweet voice said, holding a hand out to Reggie.

He shook her hand and said, "My name is Reggie."

"I know why you are here, Reggie," Mrs. Vargas said.

"You do?" Reggie said, nervously. *Oh my goodness* he thought. *She knows I have a crush on her daughter.*

"You want a job that you can do inside an air conditioned building. It is too hot out there for some of the other jobs."

"It does feel good in here," Reggie answered, not lying, but not telling the truth either about being there to be around her daughter Cynthia. "I sunburn easily," he added, pointing to his arms for some reason.

"I guess you can work with my daughter, Cynthia," Mrs. Vargas said. "Let me introduce you."

Reggie smiled.

Chapter 13

The following morning, Reggie awoke before the bell. The bell rang at seven o'clock. Breakfast began at seven thirty. Reggie awoke at a quarter to six. He showered and was at the back dining hall door at five minutes after six. The door stood open, held by an old pickle bucket half full of rocks. He announced his presence and entered the kitchen.

Mr. Vargas's forehead shone with sweat as he hefted a large pan of scrambled eggs into a warmer which would keep them hot until the campers were let into the building. Reggie peered into the warmer and saw at least twelve large pans of scrambled eggs stacked one on top of the other, each one held in place an inch above the next by a series of metal rims. He had never thought about how much food it took to feed a large group of people and what went into preparing the meal. Reggie could already tell this experience was going to be an eye opener.

"Good morning, Reggie," Mrs. Vargas called from across the kitchen. She stood before an enormous griddle with row after row of bacon and sausages popping and sizzling. "I didn't know you were coming this morning," Mrs. Vargas said as Reggie neared.

"I figured you might need the help," Reggie answered. "And we didn't really talk yesterday about what hours I would work. I'm sure I won't be able to help too much before lunch or dinner unless we have free-time."

"Well, you make a very good point, Reggie. And breakfast is the meal we need the most help with. We have four hours to get ready for lunch and five hours to get ready for dinner. If we had those kinds of hours to get ready for breakfast we would have to get here at three thirty in the morning. We get here at five thirty, but you can come once a week at a few minutes after six like today to complete your service project."

"I'll meet you every morning at five thirty unless we are on a campout or something like that."

"Oh no," Mrs. Vargas said flipping bacon pieces and sausages. A pop of grease hit Reggie in the arm and he pretended like it didn't happen, even though it did hurt a little. "You don't have to do that, Reggie."

"I want to," Reggie answered. "I'll be here."

"OK, OK," Mrs. Vargas conceded. "Cynthia is filling the syrup bottles in the dining area. Would you please go and see if she needs any help?"

"Love to," Reggie answered with a smile.

Reggie's face registered surprise as he entered the dining room to find a small group of men and women huddled around a table, obviously already finished with breakfast as their plates were pushed off to the side. Some of the men and women were sipping coffee, and they were all engaged in a serious discussion. Something about the scene seemed odd to Reggie as he had never seen any of these people besides Mr. Gary who sat at the head of the table. Mr. Gary did not see Reggie as he was engrossed in conversation with the others.

The thought of this oddity quickly faded as Reggie spied Cynthia filling the syrup containers with her back to him. He felt his forehead bead with sweat, and his tongue seemed to grow five sizes inside his mouth. Reggie took a deep breath, unclasped his clenched fists, and stepped toward her.

"Good morning," Reggie said.

Cynthia turned and Reggie had to steady himself as her hair flung around, and her scent rushed past him. "I know you," she said. "You like to eat fish sticks and Captain Crunch for dinner."

"Not really," Reggie confessed. "I hate fish sticks, and I've never eaten Captain Crunch before. My mom won't buy it. She says it has too much sugar." Reggie was surprised he didn't trip over any of his words.

Cynthia studied him. "Oh," she finally said. "I know why you picked out those things without knowing."

"You do?" Reggie asked, worried that she knew his secret.

"Yeah," Cynthia answered. "You were disoriented being away from home."

"I sure was," Reggie lied with a big smile. "I was so disoriented I even mixed up my words when I spoke to you." Reggie thought since he was lying he might just throw this excuse in as well.

"It was cute," Cynthia said.

"I'm an idiot," Reggie said.

"I don't think so," Cynthia answered. "Will you help me with these syrup containers?" she asked.

"Sure," Reggie answered.

"I'll fill them up, and if you could wipe them down when I am finished it would save me a lot of time."

"OK." Reggie did as she asked, and within a few minutes they were finished with the task.

Cynthia looked at the clock. "We have exactly one hour before the doors open," she told Reggie. "It might seem like a lot of time but we still have a bunch of stuff to do."

"OK," Reggie answered, "what's next?"

Reggie spent the rest of the morning with Cynthia learning the morning routine. He had thought before that there was so much he didn't know about what went into preparing a meal for a large group. Now he knew for a fact that there was a ton of stuff he didn't know or would have never thought about in a million years.

At seven twenty-five, just five minutes before they unlocked the dining hall doors for breakfast, Reggie rushed out the back door and ran around the building to climb the front steps to the porch. Reggie found his group and wished everyone a good morning. The group was still sleepy, but Reggie was wide awake and feeling good.

"Did you get my note?" Reggie asked Tony.

"Yes," Tony answered. "You didn't have to start your service project right away."

"I know," Reggie answered. "I just woke up early and didn't want to bother you guys. Who woke you up?" Reggie asked with a smile.

"It was Josh's turn," Tony answered.

"You OK?" Reggie asked Josh.

"Yeah," Josh answered. "I poked him in the feet. He kicked the hiking stick across the room but it didn't hit anybody. Where were you?"

Heaven, Reggie thought, but he said, "I was working on my service project."

Chapter 14

Reggie received a letter the following day. He was sure by the looks of it that it had been opened. He thought it must have been roughed up in transition and accidentally opened. The letter read:

Dear Reggie,

I miss you so much and so does Dad. He told me to tell you to make sure you are wearing your sunscreen. He thinks he is so funny, doesn't he? Ronald said to tell you hello—really, he said the other day you were actually kind of cool. He really did say it—I can explain when you get home.

How is Sally? I am sure she is OK; she is such a fine girl. You are lucky to have a friend like her. Tell her I said hello.

Sad news. I think somebody bought the vacant lot with your tree house on it. There have been some guys over there the past few days with big blueprints and lots and lots of trucks. They just look like they are getting ready to do something.

On a weird note, Mr. Jimmie stopped by yesterday and told me he forgot to give you the batteries. I had no idea what he was talking about, but I promised I would send them to you. So, that is what the batteries in the bottom of the envelope are for. He said you would know. Whatever. He was wearing a sombrero and one flip-flop when he came over. Poor man. I think he is running on half a brain or less.

I hope the food is good there. Call me when you get a chance. I love you so, so much.

Mom

Reggie looked in the bottom of the envelope and sure enough there were three AAA batteries. Reggie had forgotten he had packed the recorder and went to his trunk, dug it out and installed the batteries. He had no idea what he would use it for, but nonetheless it was ready.

That afternoon Tony signed 12UP to share the baseball field with Muddy Morning for a game of slow pitch softball. As the game began, Reggie asked Tony once again about the window in right field which seemed too close to Reggie.

"Reggie," Tony began, "nobody has ever hit that window. Would you please stop being so concerned about the window! If you hit it, I will pay for it, and I'll buy you ice cream for the rest of the summer."

Reggie smiled and said, "Deal."

The day was a scorcher for the north Georgia Mountains, and everybody was ready for the game to be over before it started. Most of Camp Timber View's property was covered with a variety of trees, but the ball field was wide open and the sun poured down on the field without any shade whatsoever. All of the kids wanted to be in the pool.

Reggie hit left-handed and threw with his right. His first time at the plate he hit a worm-burner that skipped past the third baseman and into left field. The ball rolled to the fence, and Reggie legged out a double. Tony hit after Reggie and like he had mentioned before, he gripped the bat with one hand only. Tony took two pitches, obviously waiting for a perfect pitch, and he hit a blooper over the shortstop's head. With savvy and daring base running, Reggie made it to third standing up. Sally hit next. She popped up the first pitch thrown to her into short center field. Reggie waited until the center fielder caught the ball, tagged up, and hustled toward home to try and beat the throw. One of Muddy Morning's counselors hollered at the center fielder to let him know Reggie would be running. Reggie left the bag and the ball left the center fielder's hand a split second later. All eyes were fixed on home plate. With eight feet left to home Reggie dived head first and beat the throw by a millisecond. He stood smiling with two bloody knees.

"Are you crazy?" Sissy asked him. "You have on shorts and you slid!"

Before Reggie had a chance to answer Sally chimed in saying, "If Reggie doesn't bleed during a game of anything, he doesn't feel like he tried hard enough. He bleeds when we play tennis, flag football, capture the flag, and he even somehow gets hurt when we play hide-and-seek."

"I would have been out if I hadn't slid," Reggie told Sissy. "We were down a run, and now we are tied."

"We will go up and get you cleaned up and get a few Band-Aids after the game," Tony said.

"I don't want to go in there," Reggie said with a sly grin.

"Why not?" Tony asked.

"In a few minutes they are going to be very busy in there cleaning up all the glass from the window off the floor." Reggie gave Tony another funny look.

Tony nodded his head and said, "Sure."

In the final inning the game was still tied one to one when Reggie came up to bat. He dug in at the plate and focused on the pitcher. He smashed the first pitch. The sound the ball made coming off the bat froze everyone in their shoes including Reggie. The ball arched over the first baseman and kept rising; it reached its peak over the right fielder. As the ball began its descent Reggie eyed the clinic window quickly and looked back to the ball. The ball hit the window directly in its center, and a glorious smashing, crashing sound filled the air. The ball disappeared into the clinic.

As Reggie began his victory lap around the bases he eyed Tony and said, "I like chocolate ice cream."

Reggie sat triumphantly eating a double scoop of chocolate-chocolate chip ice cream—Tony's treat. Tony sat next to him shaking his head, still not believing Reggie had actually hit the ball that far.

"You don't have to buy me ice cream all summer," Reggie said.

"Of course I do," Tony answered. "I made the bet, and I am a man of my word."

"I don't know," Reggie said hesitantly, "I'm just not comfortable with that. If I feel like every time I want an ice cream I have to find you and ask for money I just won't eat any more ice cream this summer."

"Hold on," Tony said. They were sitting in front of their cabin on a bench, and Tony hurried inside. When he emerged from the cabin he had his right fist closed tightly as he sat beside Reggie again. "You can't say no, so don't even try," Tony stated. "Hold out your hand."

Reggie held out his hand, and Tony opened his fist and put a folded fifty dollar bill in Reggie's palm.

"Oh my geez," Reggie said. "Fifty bucks! This is too much."

"I told you," Tony answered, "I won't take no for an answer." Getting up once again from the bench Tony said, "I will see you in the gym in half an hour. Remind anyone you see from our group that everyone has to be there on time. No excuses."

As Reggie entered the gym he noticed the giant royal blue curtains on the stage were drawn. He wondered what or who waited behind the curtains, and he crinkled his brow watching all of the counselors who seemed antsy. Reggie observed them counting their campers. Reggie decided it must be an incredible show, and they did not want anyone to miss it.

The gym was basically a rectangular building. It had large windows which stretched across the top of its two longer sides. At the push of a button, blinds slowly slid down and covered the windows. Another click of a different button shut off the lights, and the room was fairly dark for the middle of the afternoon.

A drum roll, obviously not real, sounded from two speakers above each side of the stage and two additional speakers from further back in the gymnasium. A succession of colorful lights flashed, joining the drum roll. A voice announced through the speakers, "Please put your hands together and help me welcome to the stage the world famous magician, Slippery Pete."

The campers clapped with wild enthusiasm, and the curtains opened. A man lay on a simple cot asleep under a pile of blankets. This was not what they expected. An electronic sign behind the man flashed the message "Boo."

All of the campers picked up on it immediately and hollered, "Booooo. Booooo. Booooo."

The man on the bed moved a bit. His head twitched. His left leg jerked up and down. His right leg shuddered violently and suddenly stopped. He rocked to the left and to the right and back and forth a few more times until the motions finally pulled him off the bed and onto the floor with a thump.

The campers had their eyes fixed to Slippery Pete. He popped up like a piece of toast out of a toaster. Slippery Pete stood with his back to the audience. He spun around suddenly, and surprise lit his face. He covered his mouth with the embarrassment of being caught sleeping in his pajamas onstage. His eyes darted around as if following something and they finally fixed just above his head. His hand readied to catch something unseen. His right arm darted out and grabbed an unseen object. Slippery Pete wrestled with it as the object pulled him this way and that. All of a sudden, like he was spiking a football, Slippery Pete slammed the unseen object to the floor.

A mushroom cloud of smoke filled the air. When it dissipated a moment later, Slippery Pete stood there in a tuxedo and a smile.

"Good evening ladies and gentlemen," he announced to the audience. "I am Pete. Some say I am a bit slippery. You might agree." He waved his arms, and another mushroom cloud of smoke filled the stage in front of him. This time when the smoke dissipated Slippery Pete was still standing there in his tuxedo—but its coloring was opposite from what they had previously observed. Before the jacket and pants had been black, and now they were white. The tie which had been white was now black. Even his shoes had switched from black to white.

Slippery Pete once again waved his arms, and an enormous blast boomed outside of the gym. Reggie swore he felt the floor move beneath him. Sally grabbed his bicep fearfully. "What was that?" she asked.

"Part of the show, I guess," Reggie answered.

"No," Sally answered. "That was outside and the show is inside."

Before Reggie had time to respond, Slippery Pete asked to no one in particular, "What was that?"

Mr. Gary came out of the audience. "Is this part of the show?" he asked Pete hesitantly.

"No," Pete answered. "I was about to turn my tuxedo different shades of purple when that monstrous noise interrupted me. Somebody better check that out. Sounded like a plane or helicopter just crashed out there." Slippery Pete tugged at his bowtie as he fidgeted.

The campers heard all of this as no one was talking, and they were extremely concerned. Mr. Gary grabbed two counselors and headed toward the exit of the gym. He opened the door an inch or so and peered out. Then, Mr. Gary and the two counselors, after a quiet conversation and a careful study of what laid beyond, slipped out the door and exited slowly.

The campers waited. For the first few minutes they remained silent, thinking they might hear something from the outside. After a few minutes and no news they began to get restless. Talking, guessing, and some worrying began.

Twenty or so minutes later the door quickly opened and closed again. Mr. Gary looked around the room and signaled for Tony to come talk with him. Mr. Gary spoke to Tony with animation and fervor. When Mr. Gary finished, he peered out the door again with care and quickly slipped out. As soon as he was gone Tony called the other counselors over and they all made a secret huddle with Tony at its center. When the huddle broke, each and every counselor looked as if they were on a mission as they returned to their groups.

Each living group gathered together separately for information and instructions. Tony and Sissy looked extremely serious. "Let me start by saying that everything is OK," Tony began. "Nobody is hurt. Nothing was destroyed. But there was an accident."

"What kind of accident?" Sally asked.

Tony started to say, "We don't..."

He was cut off by Sissy who said, "Tony! Mr. Gary said to tell them that it was an accident—and nothing more at this point." She tried to say this under her breath but everyone heard.

"It was just an accident," Tony told Sally.

"Airplane? Helicopter?" Sally asked.

"I can't say at this point," Tony answered mysteriously.

"Tell them about the papers," Sissy prodded.

"Let me tell them first what we have to do," Tony said, a little annoyed.

"Oh, right," Sissy said. "Do you want me to tell them and then you can tell them about the papers?"

"Sure," Tony said, nodding.

"Since this building is close to the accident we need to move. Some FBI, I mean, I don't know why I said that— that's not right. Some *people* are coming to take a look at what happened, and they will need to set up their headquarters in the gym. They have asked us not to go back to our cabins tonight or the dining hall. We are all going to go to the barn-hall to spend the night."

"Is that the giant barn that sticks off the side of the mountain?" Charles asked.

"Yes," Sissy answered.

"Do we have to square dance?" Mia asked.

"Not tonight," Sissy answered with a smile.

"What about clothes or sleeping bags?" Deondra asked.

"Good question," Sissy answered. "They said we could go into our cabin for three or four minutes to quickly get our sleeping bags, pillows, and to throw a few things into our backpacks. Be thinking of what you will need because they were very clear that we would only have four minutes at the most."

"Who are *they*?" Sally asked.

"The people," Sissy said blushing. "Why don't you tell them about the papers," she said to Tony changing the subject.

"Somehow during the accident, little pieces of paper were strewn everywhere. We have been asked to instruct you not to touch them—if you see one, don't look directly at it—try not to look at them at all."

"Are they laced with kryptonite?" Justin joked.

"Not funny Justin," Tony answered. "Just don't ask questions, and do as we say. Someone mentioned that they might have to send kids home who didn't follow these instructions."

"I was just kidding," Justin said holding up his hands in a surrendering pose.

"Let's go," Tony instructed. "I want a line of boys behind me, and the girls need to follow in a line behind Sissy. We will meet back up at the barn-hall in about ten minutes. There will be somebody in front of each cabin making sure you only take four minutes so be thinking what you need to pack."

"And they said no talking until we are in the barn-hall," Sissy said. "Starting now—Silence!"

12UP was the first group to leave. Other groups were still involved in deep discussions. Some girls and boys had tears in their eyes. As they exited the building both Tony and Sissy looked back at the campers behind them, put a finger to their mouths and signaled a reminder to be quiet.

Dusk was beginning to settle over the campground along with several dark rain clouds. The thick wet air washing over the campers had them all immediately sensing the turbulence in the sky above. A small parking lot sat immediately outside of the gym. It could only hold about twenty or so cars and was almost never used for this purpose. To get to it one would have to take a tiny road that snaked around the camp across several bridges. Seven black vehicles with tinted windows were parked at odd angles around the lot with no regard for the designated painted spaces. Six of the vehicles were Suburbans, and one was a Crown Vic. 12UP walked silently past the vehicles and out of the tiny parking lot. A bridge connected the parking lot with the rest of the camp, and on each end of the bridge stood two men in black suits wearing dark sunglasses. The campers walked across the bridge without the men acknowledging their existence. Just as they had passed the bridge something about one of the men struck a memory and Reggie turned back. Sally was behind him, and as Reggie walked by he noticed her eyes were wide with fear. Reggie approached the man and said, "Don't you have breakfast with..."

Before Reggie could finish his question he was cut off by the man. "Keep moving, and close your mouth," the man said rudely.

After the bridge, screened by a row of Leyland Cyprus trees was the ball field. In the center of the ball field, directly behind second base was the wreckage. A mass of twisted metal which still smoked looked to be half buried beneath the grass of the outfield. Strange lights from the craft blinked on and off changing colors with each flash of light. A buzzing type of hum came from the wreckage. It was definitely not a plane, and it was definitely not a helicopter. Sally wanted to think it was a satellite. Reggie wanted to think the same, but without speaking they both knew it was something entirely different.

Because all of the campers had been so intently focused on the wreck they only began to notice the pieces of paper after they had passed by the wreck. Little shiny silver slivers of paper were absolutely everywhere. Reggie tried not to look at them as instructed, but it was very difficult as they were everywhere. He noticed with one quick look that they had a message printed on them. After a few more steps the boys entered their cabin, and the girls continued on toward their cabin. As promised, a man was waiting in front of the cabin, and as they entered Reggie saw him check his watch.

Reggie hurriedly grabbed his sleeping bag which was already in its sack. He snatched his pillow off his bunk and stuffed it in with the sleeping bag. He tossed it toward the door and reached for his backpack. Reggie unzipped the pack and looked inside. His flashlight, poncho, canteen, and a few other items were already packed. Reggie grabbed a clean shirt, shorts, a light jacket, socks,

80

and his flip-flops. He also pushed his bathroom bag into the top of the backpack as he would not be able to go to sleep without brushing his teeth—he had his mother to thank for this habit that had been drilled into him every night of his life ever since he had teeth. As he finished, the man from outside stepped in and motioned for them all to get out.

As Reggie stepped out the door he devised a plan to get one of the pieces of paper. It came to him almost seemingly without trying. He decided he would pretend to fall down. For it to work he decided it would have to be a good fall. He decided blood would detract from any suspicions. A minute or so after they left the cabin he recognized his chance. A large branch lay across the path toward the barn-hall, and just beyond the branch bunched on the ground was a small pile of the silver papers.

When Reggie reached the branch he caught it with his right leg and sprawled toward the ground leading with his left knee. As his knee made the painful contact with the sidewalk he grabbed and tucked in his right hand a few of the slivers of paper. Tony turned to see what the commotion was, and as Reggie clutched at his knee with his left hand his right acted as if it was grabbing his back in pain. Instead of grabbing his back he was sticking the papers in his back pocket. Tony did not see as he was concentrating on Reggie's bleeding knee. He helped Reggie to his feet, and the blood ran down his leg and into his sock.

"Are you OK?" Tony whispered.

"I'm fine," Reggie whispered back. "I'm such a klutz. We can patch it up at the barn-hall. Let's go."

"Are you sure?" Tony whispered with a look of disgust at the blood. Reggie nodded and pointed for them to move on.

Tony made his way back to the front of the line and headed once again toward the barn-hall. Reggie smiled as he watched the blood drip down his leg, and he patted his back pocket knowing he had pulled off his scam.

Chapter 15

After all of the campers had gathered in the rectangular barn-hall, the different groups quickly staked their claims for territory. The back side of the building was against the mountain and did not have windows. The two shorter sides had giant open windows without screens. One of the shorter sides looked directly out to the craft shack. The other short side looked into heavy woods. The front of the building had a solid wood railing that ran the length of the structure but other than that the structure was wide open all the way to the roof. The view from the front of the building captured the road coming into the camp and trees. The distant sound of water from the falls trickled through its opening.

Even though it was not bedtime the campers set their sleeping bags and pillows up as the counselors gathered once again to talk secretively. Reggie set his up next to Sally's and wondered if Tony or Sissy would make him move. Without looking at each other they began to talk.

"What do you think is going on?" Sally asked Reggie.

"I have no idea. Do you have any idea?"

"No," Sally answered. "Whatever it is, it is weird—that is for sure."

"Did you get a good look at the wreck?" Reggie asked.

"Pretty good I guess," she answered.

"What do you think it was?"

"At first I thought it might be a satellite, but a satellite doesn't have all those weird lights, and I don't think they are that big. Are you thinking what I am thinking?" Sally asked.

"I'm afraid so, but I don't believe in UFO's. Or I didn't until now," Reggie said. "Is this really possible?"

"You wouldn't think so—until now," Sally said. "It did have that oval shape to it like the UFO's you see on sci-fi movies."

"And what about those weird guys in the black suits and sunglasses?" Reggie asked.

"I don't think they are here to get a tan," Sally said with a little smile. "And I wish I knew what those little pieces of paper said. I could tell they had words on them, but I wasn't about to risk it and pick one up."

Reggie looked around to see if anyone was listening to them. He decided that nobody was and said, "I did."

"You did what?" Sally asked, her voice a little too loud.

"Shhh!" Reggie said. He looked around and everyone was busy talking or setting up their beds. Reggie leaned over and whispered in Sally's ear, "I picked up a handful."

Sally's eyes shot open, and her mouth dropped. "What do they say?" she asked.

"I haven't looked at them yet," Reggie answered.

"How did you get them?" Before Reggie could answer Sally she said with a realization, "The bloody knee. You pretended to trip and fall and when you were down you grabbed the notes and slipped them into your pocket."

"You know me pretty well," Reggie said.

"How are you going to read them without anybody seeing?" Sally asked.

"They have to have a bathroom for us to use," Reggie answered.

"There is!" Sally said with glee. "There is a basement to this building, and they said when we got here before you did that there was a bathroom in the basement."

"Should I go now?" Reggie asked.

"Yes," Sally answered. "And after you are finished you need to flush them so you don't get caught with them."

"Good idea," Reggie said. "And by the way, did you see the four birdhouses in here? One in each corner."

Reggie found the stairs to the basement, and without looking at anyone he headed down the creaking wooden staircase. At the bottom of the stairway there were three doors; a boys' bathroom, a girls' bathroom, and a door that read, "Do Not Enter. Danger. No Admittance. Keep Out." *Wow*, Reggie thought. *Somebody does not want anyone to go in there.*

In the bathroom, Reggie locked the door and checked twice to make sure it was really locked. He fumbled nervously in his pocket to retrieve the notes and pulled them out with care as not to drop any of them into the toilet. Although the bathroom door was locked, Reggie had also locked himself into the stall as well.

A trickle of sweat dropped from Reggie's forehead to his fist as he clutched the slivers of paper. He held them in his left hand. He rubbed the back of his hand under his chin removing the droplet of sweat. Reggie took a deep breath of stale bathroom air into his lungs, coughed once, and pulled with his right index finger and thumb one of the pieces of paper free from the bunch. The message was typed and read, "The falls will stop July 31, at eleven fifty-

85

nine." He pulled another and it read, "The falls will stop July 31, at eleven fifty-nine." The next read the same as well as the next and the next and the next. All of the notes said exactly the same thing, "The falls will stop July 31, at eleven fifty-nine."

Reggie flushed all of the notes, waited for the toilet tank to fill again and flushed again just to make sure. Not knowing what to think about the message he opened the door expecting to see someone waiting to enter. The bottom of the stairwell was empty. Reggie looked again at the door reading, "Do Not Enter. Danger. No Admittance. Keep Out." The letters were all written in a brick red paint. Reggie held his ear to the door and swore he could hear the sound of machines. He heard a beep or two and then footsteps coming down the stairs. Reggie jumped away from the door and coolly walked back up the stairs nodding a hello to the boy walking down.

Back upstairs Sally eyed him as soon as he reached the top stair. Reggie tried not to look at her, but he could feel her eyes burning a hole in him. Reggie casually walked back to his sleeping bag and backpack and sat down to change his running shoes for flip-flops. As he reached into his backpack for the flip-flops he noticed out of the corner of his eye Sally pretending to find something in hers next to him. Without looking directly at each other they had another discreet conversation.

"So?" Sally asked impatiently.

"It's weird," Reggie answered.

"I didn't expect anything less," Sally answered. "What do they say?"

Reggie looked around to see if anyone was watching them, and when he determined no one was he continued. "They all say the same thing. They say 'The falls will stop July 31, at eleven fifty-nine.'"

"The falls will stop?" Sally said, not really asking a question but more or less thinking out loud.

"Yeah. All of them say exactly the same thing."

"How would the falls stop?" Sally asked.

"I guess we will have to be there July 31, at eleven fifty-nine to find out," Reggie answered.

They heard a loud pop, and when Reggie and Sally looked in the direction of the noise they saw some of the counselors setting up a portable microphone and speaker. There was a nervous energy surrounding the counselors and the campers seemed to be picking up on it as their attention turned away from their conversations and focused on their scrambling leaders.

One of the counselors named A.J. spoke into the live microphone. "Is this thing on?" The sound seemed to burst from everywhere. Before speaking into the microphone again Reggie saw someone turn a knob he hoped was the volume. "OK. First of all, thank you all so much for following the instructions given to you down in the gym and moving here in such an orderly fashion. Here is what is going to happen this evening. We are all going to pretend that this is just another normal day at camp. We are not going to talk about what happened out there," he said pointing his thumb over his shoulder. "I've heard some of the rumblings out there, and all I am allowed to say is this—it is not a UFO or a time machine or the beginning of an enemy attack." Mr. Gary, who had been standing just outside of the door talking to one of the counselors, hurried over and whispered into A.J.'s ear. A.J. nodded to Mr. Gary, turned to the group of campers and said, "And that's all I can say about that. But what I can say is that the square-dance we had planned for later in the week has been moved to tonight. We are going to have to ask you all to move your sleeping bags for the time being because we will need most of the floor for the dance. Consider your spot saved. After the dance, everyone will set their stuff back up just as it is now. OK?"

The evening turned out to be fairly uneventful. The campers were at first apprehensive about a square-dance but ended up having a blast. The music and the movements of the dances seemed to drown out the days strange happenings. Cynthia's family and the other dining hall workers set up a grill outside of the barn-hall and cooked hot dogs for dinner. They also brought baked beans, potato salad, and brownies. Cynthia's cheeks glistened with sweat as Reggie watched her lugging items back and forth to the dining hall. He offered to help, and Mr. Gary told him it was not necessary. Reggie was able to catch a word with her telling her he hoped he would be able to show up the following morning to help with breakfast. She said she hoped to see him there.

The following morning at four fifty, Reggie's watch alarm woke him. He had only been half asleep and switched it off before it woke anyone else. Before they had shut the lights off in the barn-hall the previous night, Mr. Gary told everybody on the microphone that the following morning would start a normal day. On a normal day Reggie worked in the dining hall. Without a sound he slipped out of his sleeping bag and tiptoed out the door.

Reggie awoke earlier than usual hoping to be able to make it to the ball field unseen. As he snuck out the barn-hall door and down the steps leading to the main road he smiled as he entered the foggy mountain morning. Sunrise still being two hours away, fog, and little to no moon set the perfect cover for him to take a peek at the ball field. As Reggie descended the stairs from the barn-hall he decided to make the rest of the short trip off the sidewalk and in the cover of trees just in case the guys in black suits were still around.

As Reggie made his way to a spot in the trees where he would be able to see the ball field he stopped for a moment to listen. Hearing nothing he continued to inch forward until he could see a clear view of the field. Upon his first glimpse, Reggie gasped with disbelief. The field looked brand new. The grass where the mysterious object had been in a giant hole was perfect. It was as if nothing at all had happened.

As it was still quite early, Reggie found a bench and sat. Thoughts pored through his mind as he searched for answers. Lost in his thoughts he did not realize the amount of time that had passed until he looked at his watch. Miffed, Reggie got up and walked to the dining hall.

Entering the dining hall the familiar smell of sausage, bacon, and buttery biscuits filled the air and eased Reggie's mind. Reggie nodded to Mr. Vargas who seemed surprised to see him and to Mrs. Vargas who looked as though she had expected him.

"She's in the cooler," Mrs. Vargas said to Reggie. "She probably needs help."

Reggie opened the door to the giant refrigerator and walked inside. "Hi," he said, still a little nervous by her presence.

"I didn't think you would come this morning," Cynthia said with a smile.

"Why?" Reggie asked. He wondered what she knew.

"Well," she said. "Yesterday was such a weird day around here I wondered if today would be back to normal or not."

"How was it weird for you?" Reggie asked.

"Well," Cynthia began, "I had to go to my room for like six hours yesterday, and I didn't even do anything wrong. And then when we came to work there was black paper taped to the outside of the windows."

"Really?"

"Yes, really. And when we were bringing all that food to the barn-hall, people in black suits were all over making sure we didn't look or go toward the ball field. What happened here yesterday?"

"We have all been wondering that ourselves," Reggie answered.

"We better take this stuff out of the cooler or they are going to start wondering if we froze to death in here," Cynthia said.

Reggie and Cynthia did their morning work without much more conversation until five thirty. Mr. Gary came in for his normal early breakfast with the group of people Reggie had never seen before—until today. One of the men, Reggie was certain was the man he had turned around to talk to on the bridge who told him to keep his mouth shut and keep moving.

"Help me get something out of the cooler," he told Cynthia. Inside of the cooler he pushed the door closed behind them and asked, "Who are those people who have breakfast with Mr. Gary every morning?"

"I don't know," Cynthia answered. "I don't ever see them any other time in the day. Only at breakfast when nobody else is around."

"Exactly," Reggie said, repeating words Cynthia had just said, "when nobody else is around."

"Who are they, and what are they talking about?" Cynthia asked.

"I don't know," Reggie answered, "but we are going to find out."

Chapter 16

The counselors ate their breakfasts with speed. Mr. Gary wanted to speak to all of them on the porch before the campers were allowed to leave the dining hall and go back to their cabins. The campers had not talked much, but as soon as the counselors departed the conversations erupted. With so many counselors in such a small space the night before nobody dared to talk about the mysterious events of the day or the notes found on the ground.

There had apparently been a few other brave souls besides Reggie who had somehow managed to pick up the notes. The message in the notes spread through the room like wildfire. When the counselors reentered the room, everybody knew the message written on the notes. Another topic of discussion while the counselors were out had been the door at the bottom of the stairway in the barn-hall by the bathrooms. A lot of curiosity surrounded the warnings on the door and what might lie behind.

Sissy and Tony walked back to the table and sat down. They looked annoyed. The kids all looked at each other and finally Josh asked, "What is it?"

Sissy and Tony looked at one another and Sissy nodded at Tony gesturing for him to talk. "Mr. Gary said we are not allowed to talk about what happened yesterday for now."

The group harrumphed in unison. "So let me get this straight," Deondra said, obviously annoyed. "Now we can't talk or ask about what happened yesterday or what happened the night of our campout?"

"That is correct," Tony answered.

"Instead of naming this place Camp Timber View they should have named it Camp Stupid as..."

"Watch it," Sissy cut in. "The last thing I can say about it and really shouldn't be saying at all is that in due time it will all make sense."

"I doubt it," Justin said.

"After everybody gets showered up and into new clothes we are going canoeing," Sissy announced. Tony gave her a look like the previous one she had given him. "Oh," Sissy began with apprehension. "There is an area in the middle of the lake that is marked with floating buoys and rope where you will not be allowed to go."

"For crying out loud," Deondra said. "Are we allowed to paddle the boat if we promise not to talk about it later and pretend it really didn't happen?"

Sissy looked like she might explode but when Tony laughed, she did too and the rest of the group followed in laughter at the absurdity of the situation.

When the hilarity ended Sissy said, "Mr. Gary would like to speak to all of the counselors again in the dining hall after all the campers are gone. You will have one hour of free time before we go canoeing. So, shower, change, make a phone call, whatever. We will all meet at the bridge at nine o'clock."

"You just talked to Mr. Gary," Deondra said. "Does he want to know how we took the news about being silent?"

"Deondra," Sissy said gritting her teeth. "Go take a cold shower."

As the campers in 12UP left the dining hall and started to go their separate ways Reggie called them together. Reggie looked around to make sure that no one was listening. When he was sure that nobody was, he said,

"We have to see what it is in the middle of the lake that they don't want us to see."

"I agree," said Benjamin.

"Yeah," said Bonnie. "This is all getting too weird."

"Some of us are going to need to create a diversion so somebody can paddle to the middle or swim if need be to see what it is that they don't want us to see."

"Reggie, you are a very good swimmer," Sally said. "So, I think you should be the one to either paddle in or swim in to see."

Mia spoke next which was rare. "The ropes might be placed in a way that won't let the boat inside. You could pretend to tip over or fall out and swim inside the ropes."

"That's a good idea," Reggie answered, "but how will we distract Tony and Sissy?"

Bonnie looked at Mia and said, "You could pretend to have an asthma attack, and ask Sissy to take you to the nurse to get your inhaler."

"But what about Tony?" Benjamin asked. "He will be right there."

"I know," answered Charles. "Reggie can have his canoe close to the edge of the ropes after Sissy leaves and I'll purposely tip my canoe over and call for help. When Tony comes to help me Reggie can slip out of his canoe and swim into the area that is off-limits. If you place your canoe just right, Tony would not be able to see you in the water even if he looked."

"He might notice that Reggie is not in his boat," Deondra said.

"I'll act so hysterical," Charles said, "that he will not have enough time to pay close attention to what everybody else is doing."

"Awesome," Reggie said. "I have a feeling we are going to figure out what is going on here."

The group met at the bridge at nine o'clock as previously agreed. The campers eyed one another with thoughts of their devious plan. As a group they walked in silence to the lake. They passed the ball field in silence. The grass where the strange object had landed was perfect and green like nothing had ever happened. Nobody said a word.

At the lake the kids paired up and put on life jackets. There was a cloud of nervousness hanging over the group and Tony and Sissy noticed.

"Are you guys all right?" Sissy asked.

Sally took control saying, "We are just fine. We talked as a group this morning when you and Tony were talking to Mr. Gary and some of us were just a little concerned with the recent happenings. It *has* been weird. We are fine now. I promise." Sally had a thought. "We were all actually concerned about Mia."

"Why were you concerned about Mia?" Sissy asked.

"She was having trouble breathing earlier," Sally answered.

"Oh," Sissy answered.

"It's nothing to worry about," Sally said, glad she had put the thought into Sissy's mind.

The campers teamed up in twos and headed out in their canoes. Charles paired with Josh and Mia paired with her best friend Olivia. Reggie and Sally were first out and waiting near the boundary for the diversion. All of the other pairings left Tony to pair with Sissy.

As they were about to get into a boat together and head out into the lake Mia and Olivia's boat came back toward the dock. "I... I... can't...breathe...very... well," Mia said as they pulled their boat beside Tony and Sissy's boat. "I... think... I... am... having... an... asthma... attack."

"Oh my gosh," Sissy said, jumping out of the canoe. "You need your inhaler." Sissy grabbed Mia's arm and rushed her off toward the clinic.

As Sissy and Mia walked out of eyesight, Reggie gave Charles a thumbs-up. Tony had not had time to regroup when Charles tipped his boat on purpose and flailed wildly in the water. Tony dove headfirst and swam wildly toward Charles.

Sally and Reggie were sitting in the boat next to the ropes and the buoys. When Sally saw Tony dive into the water and head toward Charles she said, "Now!"

Reggie had been waiting for her signal, and he slipped into the water on the other side of the boat. As Tony swam toward Charles, Reggie swam into the out of bounds area. Immediately inside the area he understood the secret. Reggie felt around in a few different areas to make sure and then made his way back to the canoe.

After lunch the group had an hour of free-time. Reggie and Sally whispered to each member of the group that he would let them in on his discovery at that time.

They met at a secluded spot behind the barn-hall. Reggie had noticed a trail leading up the hill behind the barn-hall the night the unidentified object crash landed into the ball field and the campers had to spend the night. The trail led a hundred yards or so up the hill and flattened out at an area which suddenly appeared with an enormous exposed rock face. An area as large as a roller rink was nothing but rock. The dirt and trees suddenly stopped and started once again on the other side of the rock face.

Once everybody was there and settled Reggie gathered his thoughts. He had not even told Sally what he had found. There had not been a time where it would have been safe.

"I'm dying here," Sally said. "What was under there?"

"Well," Reggie began. "There was no magic or supernatural cause of what we saw with Mr. George. They have weighed down a dock so that it is just below the surface of the water. Each of the four corners of the dock has a chain which I imagine must be attached to an anchor to hold it below the surface of the water."

"Oh my goodness," Mia said.

"So somebody can stand on it or sit in a rocking chair like Mr. George was and it looks like they are standing or sitting on top of the water," Olivia said with amazement.

"That is so wrong," Bonnie commented. "Why would somebody do that?"

"We are being messed with," Charles put forth.

"I think so," Reggie answered.

"But why?" Sally asked.

"That is what we have to find out," Reggie answered. "I think it is important that we don't act like we know anything. Whatever they are doing, Tony and Sissy must be in on it. We don't want to make them suspicious."

"Reggie is right," Sally agreed. "Something strange is obviously going on and Tony and Sissy have to be a part of it. If they didn't know they would be as freaked out as we all are. And they are most probably getting their instructions from Mr. Gary."

"I think it is very important," Reggie said, "that we don't tell any of the other groups what we know. Are we all in agreement?" Reggie looked around the group as all the heads nodded. "If you agree to act in secrecy as a group raise your hand." Everybody raised their hand.

The impromptu meeting ended, and everyone scattered except Sally. The two looked at each other and smiled like only best friends do, understanding without saying what each person is feeling.

They began to descend the mountain when Reggie noticed another trail leading to the bottom which veered off from the other one. The other trail was fairly grown over, but for some reason Reggie decided to take it. At one point on the trail a clear view of the barn-hall's roof came into view with absolute clarity. What Reggie and Sally saw mystified them.

"What do you think they are?" Sally asked.

"I have no idea, but I am sure they have something to do with whatever is going on at this camp."

"At our next meeting we have to show the rest of the group this stuff. Maybe one of them will know what they are."

As they walked on, Reggie felt a pang of guilt thinking about the pact his group had made just moments before because he knew what he was about to do next would go against this very pledge of secrecy. Luckily, to ease his mind, he had not raised his own hand.

Chapter 17

The next morning Reggie arrived at the dining hall earlier than usual. In his left hand he held a plastic grocery store bag behind his back. The Vargas family had not arrived, and Reggie waited by the back door with a lump in his throat. He had a plan and hoped Cynthia would go along. Without her he was sure it would not work.

When the Vargas family arrived they were not really surprised to see him. Reggie had been such a loyal and energetic worker that his early arrival was not in the least suspicious.

When Mr. and Mrs. Vargas had gone inside along with their son, Reggie signaled for Cynthia to stay behind.

"What's going on?" she asked.

"I need your help," Reggie said. "Something very weird is going on and you can help me figure out what it is."

"OK," Cynthia said.

"Yesterday when all of the counselors stayed in the dining hall after lunch and the campers left, did you happen to hear what they were talking about?" Reggie asked.

"No," Cynthia answered. "It was so weird. I was just working and doing my normal chores and Mom told me I had to go to my room for one hour. I asked her what I had done wrong and she said nothing. When I tried to argue with her she just told me to be quiet and go to my room."

"Do you agree with me that something very weird is going on at this camp?" Reggie asked.

"Yes," Cynthia said with conviction.

"Will you help me figure out what is going on?" Reggie asked.

"Yes," Cynthia answered.

"What if what you have to do puts you in danger?" Reggie asked.

"If it makes my life exciting, I'm in," Cynthia answered.

Reggie took from his back pocket and held up for her to see the digital recorder Mr. Jimmy had given him. "I want to tape this to the bottom of the table where Mr. Gary sits every morning with those people we have never seen."

"How?" Cynthia asked.

Reggie unclenched his fist which had been gripping the plastic grocery bag and pulled out a roll of duct tape. "I found this in our cabin. I guess you could say I am borrowing it from Tony without him knowing." Reggie paused to think. "I figure if I put three to five pieces of this over the recorder to the underside of the table being careful not to cover the microphone, it will stay for at least an hour."

"The people who sit with Mr. Gary usually only stay for thirty to thirty-five minutes," Cynthia said. "Do you think it will pick up their conversation?"

"I don't know," Reggie answered. "I have never used the recorder. I hope so."

"Why don't you get to work on taping it to the underside of the table," Cynthia suggested. "I'll sprinkle some Cheerios on the floor around the table so if my mom or dad comes in you could pretend you were picking up a spill. Also, if they come out into the dining room I will do a pretend sneeze really loud," Cynthia said.

"OK," Reggie answered. "Should I go ahead and start recording?" Reggie asked. "They'll be here in fifteen to twenty minutes."

"I think you should wait," Cynthia suggested.

"OK," Reggie agreed.

Reggie and Cynthia went about their morning work as if it were any other day. Reggie had his eye on the kitchen clock waiting to go push the record button on the digital recorder. In his mind he had selected a time and just as it arrived Mr. Vargas asked for his help carrying a large container of trash to the dumpster. Reggie had no other option than to agree and help. As they were heaving and dumping the heavy container into the dumpster Reggie saw out of the corner of his eye Mr. Gary enter the dining hall with his group. His plan was going to fail.

After they dumped the can, Reggie told Mr. Vargas there was something he forgot to do and ran back toward the building. As he entered the dining hall out of breath, Cynthia met him at the door holding her hand up with a smile.

"I pushed the record button," she said.

Before he could even think about what he was saying, Reggie said, "I could just kiss you."

"Maybe later," Cynthia said, smiling as she walked off to tend to more of her duties.

Reggie's heart did flips. He was full of a bevy of different emotions. His nerves fluttered with the idea that the recorder was under Mr. Gary's table recording the conversation. His heart pounded with the knowledge that Cynthia might accept a kiss. His nerves shuddered with worry as he had never kissed a girl before. Reggie's head was spinning so wildly he didn't know what to do.

"Are you OK Reggie?" Mrs. Vargas asked. "You look a little flushed."

"I've never been better," Reggie answered.

As soon as Mr. Gary left the building with his group, Reggie removed the recorder from beneath the table. He stashed the recorder back in his plastic grocery bag and stuck it behind a sack of rice in the stockroom. He did not have time to check to see if it worked as the campers were due to begin breakfast shortly.

After finishing his duties, Reggie grabbed the bag with the recorder and headed to meet his group on the dining hall's front porch. His stomach turned with excitement. He did not think he could wait until after breakfast to listen to whatever the recorder might have captured and quickly devised a plan.

"Tony," he said weakly. "Do you mind if I go lie down while you all eat breakfast? I don't feel so well."

"Sure, buddy," Tony answered. "Do you want me to take you to the nurse?"

"No," Reggie answered. "I think a quick nap will make everything all right."

"OK. After breakfast we have free time for an hour so you will be able to get in a good nap. I'll tell the rest of the guys to be real quiet if they have to go back in the cabin."

Reggie thanked Tony and turned toward the cabin. He almost broke into a run but decided it would not look as though he was sick if he ran away. Reggie walked to the corner and once out of sight sprinted to his cabin. He pulled the screen door so hard it slammed violently against the side of the cabin. Reggie climbed the bunk in two quick steps and plopped down on his mattress out of breath.

Hands trembling he pulled the recorder out of the plastic grocery bag and pushed play. The sound quality was not great but it was pretty good. Reggie could understand every word. At first Mr. Gary was talking about the eggs and how they were especially good or he was especially hungry. A couple of the other people talked about the rain expected later in the day and the Atlanta Braves game the night before. The manager of the team, Bobby Cox, was thrown out of the game for arguing with the umpire, and one of the guys thought it was hilarious. When they mentioned *his* name, Reggie almost fell off of the bed. One of the men said, "I think Reggie is on to us. He was at the lake yesterday and got out of his boat and crossed the restricted area and touched the sunken dock. We need to keep a close eye on him."

Reggie could not believe what he had just heard. He rewound the recording and listened to it again and again. How did they know his name? How had they seen him swim into the restricted area? Who were these people? Reggie listened to the rest of the recording but there was nothing else said that was important. Reggie stuffed the recorder under his mattress and hightailed it back to the dining hall. He needed to call another meeting, pronto.

Just as he reached the dining hall porch the group was coming out the dining hall. Tony walked out first, and surprise filled his face as he spotted Reggie.

"I thought you didn't feel well?" Tony said.

Reggie motioned for Tony to come closer so he could tell him a secret. Whispering into Tony's ear Reggie said, "I went to the bathroom, and I feel fine now." Reggie felt awful for lying but he also felt it was necessary to get to the bottom of the mystery at hand.

103

"Oh," Tony said, nodding with understanding. "I am glad you feel better."

Reggie told Sally in her ear they needed to have another secret meeting and to pass the word to the group. He said they would meet in the same spot as before in thirty minutes. Reggie needed to gather his thoughts before the meeting and talk with Sally.

When the group scattered, Reggie told Sally what he heard on the recordings and how he was concerned that someone was watching him.

"How would they have seen you?" Sally asked, concern filling her face.

"I don't know. I know Tony didn't see me in the water. He could not have told them. Even though, I still don't trust him to tell him the information or ask him what is going on. He and Sissy have to be in on this game or whatever it is."

"Do you think someone was watching you from the woods?"

"It's possible."

Thirty minutes later the group met at the secluded spot behind the barn-hall. When Reggie arrived they were all sitting in a semicircle waiting for him. A worried feeling seemed to hang in the air.

"Are you all right, Reggie?" Bonnie asked. "Tony said you skipped breakfast because you were not feeling well."

"I'm fine. I just needed some time alone to listen to something." Reggie told them about the digital recorder he brought to camp and how he had used it to listen in to Mr. Gary's conversation. Reggie left out the part of how he had used Cynthia's help. He felt since they didn't know her like he did that they might not trust her.

"So, how do you think they saw you?" Olivia asked.

"They probably have somebody watching us from the woods," offered Benjamin.

"No, I think they are more sophisticated than that," said Charles.

"Maybe they have cameras hidden all over camp," said Sally.

"Wouldn't we be able to see those?" Charles asked.

"Oh my goodness!" Reggie yelled. "They do have cameras! They do!"

"Where?" asked Sally.

"The birdhouses! They are not really birdhouses. They have to be cameras and that explains why they are everywhere—even three and four of them inside every building."

"I think he is right," Deondra said. "The birdhouses are cameras."

"How are they seeing with them? Where are the wires?" Josh asked.

Charles thought and said, "They must be wireless. There must be some place on site where they are secretly gathering all of the information. They must have transmitters and receivers and stuff like that."

"I think they do," Sally said. "Is it OK if I show them?" she asked Reggie.

"Sure."

The group stood and followed Sally. She led them down the overgrown trail she and Reggie had previously taken. When a view of the barn-hall roof came into view they all froze as one. Atop the roof, hidden from any other vantage point were antennas, satellite dishes, wires, metal pieces pointing this way and that and a number of never before seen devices. After they had taken it all in, without speaking Sally motioned for them all to return to their meeting place up on the mountain.

When they were back at their secret meeting place their eyes searched the group and finally all eyes landed on Reggie. Noticing all of their eyes on him he had a sudden realization. They all thought of him as their leader. Reggie had never been a leader before—until now he had always been a follower. A contributor, but a follower nonetheless. Reggie decided in this moment he could look at the ground and let somebody else take the reins of leadership or he could step up and take it himself.

He decided to take it himself. Reggie looked at Sally and she gave him a nod.

"All right," he began. "Once again I have to say how important it is that we do not tell anybody what we know. Not Tony, not Sissy, not anybody." As their new leader Reggie felt obligated to tell them about Cynthia. He felt it was important to be an honest leader. "I have had to enlist the help of one other person to get some of the information I have gathered, but I assure you she will not tell a soul, and she is as in the dark about what is going on as we are. If we as a group decide she should not know what we know, I will not tell her anything more. I think she can be of some help to us though." Reggie told them more about Cynthia and took a vote. They voted unanimously to bring her into the group. Reggie was thrilled and relieved. "I guess we all now know what the door at the bottom of the barn-hall door leads to—the one that reads, 'Do Not Enter. Danger. No Admittance. Keep Out.'"

"Must be the command center," Charles said.

"I bet it's full of computers and television monitors and high tech stuff like that," Sally offered.

Mia asked, "Why do you think they are watching us?"

"Good question," Reggie answered. "Any ideas?"

"To make sure we behave," Benjamin said.

"No," Sally answered. "It has to be expensive to do this, and I haven't seen any reason to have all of this for behavior reasons."

"Maybe they are making a movie. A documentary of camp life," Josh said.

"What do you think?" Reggie asked Mia. Reggie realized that Mia was a deep thinker who rarely spoke, but when she did her thoughts were very valuable.

"I think they are making a reality show," Mia answered. "It seems like most shows on television these days are reality shows. And none of us paid to come here. We somehow won a trip here. Seems suspicious to me. I saw my mom reading all of those papers that came with the free ticket and she and my dad had an argument about something the papers said. Maybe our parents know what is going on here." Mia hung her head with self doubt. "Just a thought," she said.

"That makes a lot of sense," Reggie said. Mia smiled sheepishly. "So, let's get this straight. So far we think that the birdhouses are cameras. We think they might be filming a reality show. The people in charge might think that I am on to something. And Tony and Sissy are definitely in on the scam."

Everybody nodded their heads in agreement.

"Then," Reggie continued, "they wanted us to pick up the little notes the day of the mysterious crash into the ball field. Why? Why would they want us to pick up and read those notes?" As Reggie asked this he looked at Mia.

"They want to see what we do about it," Mia answered. "Maybe it is the final episode of the show. They want us to be really freaked out, and they will somehow reveal how they fooled us all summer and that we are on some crazy reality show. It is a gotcha moment for them."

"What we need to do is make it a gotcha moment for *them*," Sally said.

"I agree," Reggie answered. "So, here is what we need to do between now and when the falls are supposed to stop. Pretend everything is normal. Do not look directly at the birdhouses or act like we know in any way that they are cameras. Let's also assume the cameras have microphones, and this is our only safe spot to talk. And, most importantly, be thinking of what we can do to get them instead of them getting us."

"Does anybody think it would be possible to get into the room at the bottom of the barn-hall?" Charles asked.

"I bet there is somebody in there twenty-four hours a day watching monitors and stuff like that," Olivia said.

"We could pull the fire alarm," Sally put forth.

"It's a possibility," Reggie said. "If we are going to look in there, the best time to do it would be the early morning when all those strangers are at the breakfast meeting. I bet if they leave anybody in there it is just one person."

The camp bell rang signaling free time was over. The members of 12UP looked at each other knowingly and walked down the hill.

Chapter 18

Tony and Sissy announced that the day's activities would be had at the ropes course on the other side of the mountain. The campers tried not to stare at the birdhouses along the entirety of the trail to the course. The group, including Tony and Sissy were unusually quiet—all seemingly deep in thought.

The first exercise involved three pedestals which were about four feet off the ground and one, six foot board. The pedestals were about five feet apart. The first pedestal had plenty of room for a group of twelve to fifteen kids to stand on comfortably. The second pedestal had room for about eight, and the last had room for five. The object of the game was to get all of the campers from the first pedestal to the third without anyone touching the ground. After Tony and Sissy told the group the rules they backed away to watch. As they did, the group looked to Reggie.

As the newly appointed unspoken leader, Reggie had many ways he could go with his style of leadership. He had thought about this on the hike up to the ropes course. He could be a dictator like Coach Steve—it was his way or the highway. Coach Steve gave orders and everybody listened. Reggie was not fond of the Coach. He could go completely the other way and be like Mr. Davies his science teacher who wanted everybody to like him and did just about whatever the group wanted to do. Reggie hated his class. He felt as if he was on a rudderless ship when in his class. With no certain direction they only floated this way and that it seemed. Or he could be like his art teacher, Mr. Cain—different every day according to the needs of the class.

Mr. Cain could go from your funny, fun loving friend to a tough disciplinarian in the drop of a hat. He could give you a high five one minute and a timeout the next. Reggie adored him. Mr. Cain did not play favorites. From his own mouth, Mr. Cain said he believed in every one of his students. They were all unique, all special, and all worthy of great things if they would put in the work and believe in themselves. As Reggie thought about it on the hike up, Mr. Cain was more like a guide. He recognized what the class needed at a particular moment and provided. When the class needed a tyrant to find order he ruled with an iron fist. When the class rolled with ease he sat in the backseat and enjoyed the ride. Most of the time, Mr. Cain switched between styles and approaches as easily as one wave in the ocean gives way to the next. If Reggie was going to be like any leader he knew it was Mr. Cain.

Reggie surveyed the group. He knew what they should do first, but he wanted to hear it come out of one of their mouths. He decided to lead the conversation as Mr. Cain might. "So?" he asked. "What should we do first?"

"The heaviest people should go first," Benjamin offered. Reggie had thought this same thing.

"Why?" Reggie asked.

"They can stand in the center of the second pedestal, and the lighter people can balance on the edges and hold on to the people in the center."

"Great idea," Reggie praised. "Let's try it."

One of the girls laid the board in between the two pedestals, and four of the heaviest members of the group crossed—all boys. They looked to Reggie to cross as all of the girls weighed less than him but he did not.

"The girls need to go now," he said.

"But you are heavier than us," Sally said.

"I know," Reggie answered, "but whoever goes last will have to hang on to somebody and pick up the board with one arm and hand it across the group so we can go to the next pedestal."

"Good thinking," Sally answered.

As Reggie stood on the second pedestal, he gripped Josh's hand with his own and handled the board with the other. He thought again of Mr. Cain. *He always praises us when we do well. It always makes me feel like I can do even better.*

"You guys are doing awesome," Reggie said as he passed the board over his head across the group. "What now?"

"Let's do the same thing again," Justin suggested.

"It won't work," Reggie answered. "I'm barely hanging on here and that platform is much smaller."

"We could make a pyramid or something over there," Deondra said.

"That is a good idea," Reggie answered, "but I don't think there is enough room for error. One false move and we will have to start all over."

For a full minute nobody said a word. Reggie had an idea but continued to wait for another two full minutes. When he felt enough time had passed he said, "Let's try this. Mia, Olivia, and Bonnie are on the edge facing the third pedestal. You three go over there now which will give us room to move around here." The three girls carefully walked across the board to the third pedestal. "Now," Reggie continued. "Charles, Justin, and Josh will go over one at a time and each put one of the girls on their shoulders. This way two people can take up the space of one."

Charles carefully crossed to the third pedestal, and Olivia and Bonnie helped Mia get atop the shoulders of Charles. Justin crossed next. Olivia was a tiny girl and Justin easily got her on his shoulders and stood. As directed by Reggie, Sally and Benjamin crossed next. Somehow, Sally helped Bonnie get on Benjamin's shoulders. Benjamin was not a strong boy and began to falter immediately. His knees wobbled, and his face showed fear. Reggie recognized it immediately and shouted encouragement.

"Hold on Ben," he yelled. "You can do it. Just give us less than five minutes, and this will be over."

"OK," Benjamin whimpered.

Reggie sent Josh across next. Olivia and Mia, who sat on Charles's and Justin's shoulders helped pull Sally up onto Josh's shoulders. This left Deondra and Reggie.

"This isn't going to work," Sally called. "There is only room for maybe one more person. Maybe half of a person if they hold on to someone here, but definitely not two people."

Reggie smiled. "I guess we will have to come over as one person," he said. Reggie squatted down and motioned for Deondra to climb onto his shoulders. She did and Reggie raised his hands for her to grab. Deondra grabbed Reggie's hands and squeezed with all her might as Reggie strained to stand upright with her straddling his shoulders. His first attempt to stand upright was unsuccessful as she was just too heavy. "It's not going to work," he said.

"Yes it is," Deondra answered. "I am going to count to three and jump as high as I can. When I say three you are going to stand up as fast as you can. I think if you can get just little help from my jump it will work. Do you trust me?"

"Yes," Reggie answered with a smile. "Let's do it."

Deondra counted out loud. "One, two, three." On three she jumped as high as she ever had in her life, and Reggie sprung from his crouched stance like a tiger. When the two bodies met, Reggie had enough of his legs under him to continue to a standing position. Those who had free hands to clap on the third pedestal did so, and the others just sighed and smiled.

"Now what?" Deondra asked Reggie.

"Now we walk across the board," he answered. "Hold your arms out like you are an airplane," Reggie instructed. "Stay as still as you can. Pretend in your mind that we together are one piece." Deondra actually closed her eyes as she stuck her arms out. Her legs clasped against Reggie's back, she tilted her head back to where she felt completely balanced. As she breathed in and out steadily, Reggie put one foot in front of the other and crossed the beam without trouble. Safely on the other side, Deondra opened her eyes and grabbed Sally. They did it! All ten of them on the tiny pedestal, directed by none other than Reggie.

Chapter 19

Reggie waited on the back dock the next morning for the Vargas family. He could not sleep and had been waiting for at least thirty minutes when they arrived. Reggie had played his brain's movie of the previous day over and over, again and again in his mind. He was unsure of what the group decided in their secret meeting spot the night before and what he was about to ask Cynthia to do.

When her parents had entered the dining hall and were out of earshot she said, "You're up to something. I know that look on your face."

Reggie peered out into the dining area and saw the birdhouses perched in the corners. Next, he looked around the kitchen area and did not see any birdhouses, but decided to play it safe. "Will you help me get the sausage patties out of the cooler for your mom?" Reggie asked.

Inside the safety of the cooler Reggie told Cynthia all of the latest news. Cynthia's eyes widened with each new piece of information. When Reggie finished he was out of breath as he was talking as fast as he possibly could. Mrs. Vargas would wonder in another minute what they were doing.

"Here is what I need you to help me with today," Reggie said, still speaking a mile a minute. "Sally is going to try and see what is behind the door at the bottom of the barn-hall stairs. Mr. Gary usually shows up at six fifteen with his group. Charles is going to pull the fire alarm at six twenty-three so Mr. Gary's group has a chance to settle in at their table. Sally will be hiding in the girls' bathroom at the bottom of the stairs waiting for someone to exit the door. Hopefully, because it is so early and they will be panicked, they will leave the door unlocked. You and I are

114

going to block both dining hall doors with tables." Reggie took a breath and continued. "I am going to spill a canister of orange juice in between the two doors after they walk in. As soon as I spill it I need you to help me move the tables out of the way so I can mop it up. We will move the tables in front of each of the doors. So, if an alarm goes off and Mr. Gary wants to respond, the tables will slow him down and give Sally enough time to peek into the room."

"Sounds like a plan," Cynthia said, tossing Reggie a package of sausages. "Did you sleep any last night?" she said, with a deep smile.

"Not much," Reggie answered.

They arrived at six twenty. As soon as Mr. Gary and his crew walked in, Reggie grabbed a large container of orange juice and headed for the doors. When he was equally between the two doors he tripped himself and dumped the container of sticky juice on the floor. Reggie made sure the juice went all over so it would take time to clean. As soon as it did he called Cynthia over to help him move the tables out of the way so he could clean it up. They put the tables in front of the doors, three deep.

A moment later, Reggie and Cynthia heard the distinct noise of an alarm in the distance. Reggie's eyes immediately went to Mr. Gary. At first he didn't hear it as he was making small talk with Mr. Vargas. When Reggie noticed Mr. Gary's head twitch and then turn he knew he had heard. Reggie immediately dipped the mop into the mop bucket, and without ringing it out he slung water on top of the orange juice. Reggie turned his back to Mr. Gary and pretended not to hear the alarm.

As Mr. Gary ran toward the exit he noticed the blocked doors and the mess on the floor. Surveying the situation with three tables obstructing each door and orange juice and water on the floor he decided to turn around and go through the kitchen and out the back door. Reggie thought he would wait for him to clean the floor and clear the way. When he turned and ran through the kitchen, Reggie hoped Sally and Charles would not get caught. After a moment's hesitation, Reggie began running after him.

When Reggie could see the back door he almost busted out laughing aloud as he saw Cynthia standing in front of it with it shut and locked. Mr. Gary tried to open the door, but it could not be opened without the key.

"Open the door," Mr. Gary demanded.

"No," Cynthia answered. "It's not safe. I saw a coyote sniffing around the dumpster."

"When we open the door it will scare the coyote off," Mr. Gary said.

"I gave the key back to my dad," Cynthia answered.

"I don't have it," Mr. Vargas said. "You didn't give it back to me."

"Oh," Cynthia said. "Maybe I left it in the stock room. I went to get some oatmeal right after I locked the door. I'll check." As Cynthia walked to the stockroom she caught Reggie's eye and gave him a secretive wink. Reggie almost doubled over with laughter but somehow held it in.

"Reggie," Mr. Gary said, "help me move the tables by the front door. I'll go that way."

"I think those doors are locked with the same key," Reggie answered, trying to stall a little more.

"I just came in the door a few minutes ago," Mr. Gary said.

"Oh," Reggie answered. "Right."

At the barn-hall, Charles pulled the alarm and ran up into the woods and out of sight. As he did this, Sally had the girls' bathroom door cracked at the bottom of the stairs across from the door she hoped someone would run out. As Sally waited in the dark she could hear her heart pounding. As soon as the alarm sounded she heard movement from the room across the hall. She immediately heard locks clicking and soon after the door flew open and a man ran up the stairs.

As soon as the man reached the halfway point up the stairway, Sally crept out of the bathroom and peeked in the door. On her first glimpse she looked for another person, and when she did not see one she then took in the room. There must have been a hundred television screens she thought; one for each birdhouse. Computers, printers, fax machines, copiers, desks, and phones. The room looked like a NASA control center Sally had seen in a movie. On one of the desks she saw a name plate which read "Gary Slidell" and Sally assumed it was Mr. Gary's desk. She put the last name in the back of her head for something she wanted to do later. With one last look, Sally reentered the bathroom and hid again.

When Mr. Gary arrived at the barn-hall he bent and grabbed his knees trying to catch his breath. The man who had been in the control center below met him at the door. The alarm blared still as they tried to speak to one another.

"What is going on?" Mr. Gary asked.

"I have no idea," the man answered. "There isn't any smoke anywhere. It must be a faulty alarm."

As soon as the man finished speaking, Mr. Gary heard the fire trucks. "Great," he said.

When Sally heard the sirens she froze. The firemen would search the building for any signs of fire, and they would of course find her. Her mind raced for a solution.

117

Sally knew she would not be able to make it up the stairs undetected. She decided there was no way Mr. Gary would let the firemen into the control center. They might blow the cover off whatever it was that was going on at the camp. It was a gamble she had to take and she did. As soon as she made her decision she ran back into the control center and hid in a cabinet. A moment later someone came down the stairs and locked the door from the outside. Luckily, it was the kind of door Sally could unlock from the inside when she was ready to leave. Outside of the door she could hear a conversation.

"You may not go into this room," she heard Mr. Gary say.

"I need to see if there is anything in there that might have set off the alarm," the second voice answered.

"I assure you there is nothing in there that set off the alarm," Mr. Gary said.

"Fine," the second voice said. "If you don't want me to go in there it is fine but you will need to look in there while I check the bathrooms."

"Great," Mr. Gary answered.

Sally heard the locks click once again, and she felt a presence as Mr. Gary entered the room. As he did she heard him let out a sigh of relief. From a tiny crack in the cabinet she could see a sliver of him. Mr. Gary reached into his pocket and pulled out his cell phone.

"Bill," Mr. Gary said. "Where are the firemen?" Mr. Gary listened. "Good," he said to whatever the voice on the other line had said. "Don't let them go up the hill to look at the building. They might see all of our equipment on the roof." He listened again. "Good," he answered to whatever was said, "I'm coming up."

When Mr. Gary left the room he locked the door. Sally had a crazy idea and after wavering for a moment she decided to act on the thought. With her decision she ran over to one of the laptop computers and clicked on the icon to get on the Internet. Once on the Internet she googled the name "Gary Slidell." There were one thousand plus results. Sally clicked on the first link which looked promising. The webpage popped up on the screen, and Sally read what came as no surprise. Mr. Gary, otherwise known as Gary Slidell, was a television executive at a major television network. He began his career with gritty police dramas and made a name for himself with his creativity in reality television programming. There was absolutely no doubt now about what was going on.

Sally clicked off the Internet and moved to the door. She put her ear to the door and holding her breath she unlatched the lock. Sally slowly pulled the door open and when she did not see anyone standing on the other side she ran back into the bathroom to hide once again. Not a moment too soon as once she crouched behind the door once again she heard footsteps coming down the stairs. Sally peeked through the crack in the door and recognized the man who had originally run out of the door. Since he did not know that Mr. Gary had locked the door he did not think it strange that the door was left open. He entered the door, and Sally heard the locks click into place. Unsure of whether she should stay a little longer or go, her heart fled to her throat as she heard another set of footsteps coming down the stairs.

It was Reggie. "Sally," he whispered.

Sally emerged from behind the door. With the intensity of the moment and the release of her anxiety,

Sally sprang from her hiding spot and wrapped her arms around Reggie with a massive hug.

"Let's go," he said in her ear.

Together they crept up the stairs and out the door.

Outside the barn-hall, Reggie and Sally both breathed a great sigh of relief as the fire trucks disappeared over the ridge of the road. Sally sniffed the morning air, looked at Reggie, and said, "You smell like orange juice."

Chapter 20

Sally told the group all she had learned in the basement of the barn-hall after breakfast. It had quickly become an unwritten rule that they would meet in their secret location at the beginning of every free time. Reggie introduced their newest member, Cynthia, at the beginning of the meeting, and she was greeted with hugs all around.

When Sally finished speaking, Benjamin said what the entire group was thinking when he said, "I can't believe this is happening. This is just the craziest thing ever."

"I think it's great," Mia said. "If I was at home, my mom would be shuffling me back and forth between guitar lessons, soccer practice, Sunday school, and the library to get stacks of books for the summer reading program. This is awesome—we are going to be on a television program!"

All of the kids smiled. "I agree," Reggie said when nobody else spoke. "If we can decide to look at this the right way, it is like we have been given a cool gift. We can go two ways here. We can either be upset that we have been tricked and pout about it—as my mom would say. Or, we see it as the opportunity of a lifetime. When we all go back to our schools in the fall we will be television superstars," Reggie said half-joking.

The group laughed as one at the joke and the thought of being popular for even a moment. For some of them, the idea of being popular was as far off as the possibility of being invited to Willy Wonka's factory for a tour.

"Being popular isn't that great," Charles confessed. "Believe me, I am not bragging, but at my school I am considered popular. A lot of times I wish I wasn't," he said, looking dejected.

"Why?" Bonnie asked. "I would love for just one day to be popular."

"Me too," Cynthia said, speaking for the first time to the group. "Sometimes people don't even give me a chance because I am from a different country. I dream of being popular."

"I can never let my guard down," Charles answered. "I feel like I always have to wear the right clothes and be in a good mood and talk only to the other popular people." Charles paused; a disgusted look crossed his face. "Sometimes I would like to have a bad day. Sometimes, I would like to wear my old, no name brand clothes which are so comfortable. I would like to talk to who I want to without being questioned by the other popular kids. Come to think of it," Charles said, "being popular stinks most of the time. I have never had as much fun as I have had this summer just being one of the gang. You guys are so great. Thanks."

Reggie waited again for somebody to speak and when they did not he said, "Charles, we could not have done it without you. You are a smart guy. You deserve all the good things that come with being popular—some people don't—but you do. Don't ever feel bad about it again. If you do," Reggie paused and smiled a giant mischievous grin, "just remember that you were a very equal part of 12UP."

"Thanks," Charles answered, he was obviously touched with emotion.

"Now," Reggie continued, "we have two more days until Sunday when the falls are going to supposedly stop. What are we going to do?"

"We could not show up," Deondra put forth.

"That's no fun," Sally answered. "We have to do something that will make Mr. Gary and all of the TV people behind this come out from behind the cameras and expose themselves instead of us being exposed as unknowing players in this game. We have to do something that will shock them enough to come running out on camera scared for our lives."

"I think I may have an idea," Cynthia said. "I need to talk to my cousin first before I promise anything."

"What is it?" Reggie asked.

"I don't want to say in case it doesn't work," Cynthia answered. "You all keep thinking of ideas. I am going to make a phone call, and I will let you know what I come up with, tomorrow after breakfast."

Intrigued as they all were, the meeting broke up. The day's events called for the group's second campout and they all hoped they would not have shenanigans like at the first one. Tony and Sissy instructed them to all go and pack their backpacks for a night out. They would be hiking to a different campground than before. There was another division of Camp Timber View called the pioneer division. The pioneer division ended their summer a few days prior and their camp was empty. Reggie, Sally, and the rest of the crew wondered what was in store for them at this location.

When the group arrived at the pioneer camp, a large fire blazed in the center of a large playing field. It was twelve noon. Fires were dramatic and meaningful at midnight, not noon. The size of this fire would be meaningful at any time of day. The members of 12UP had peeled eyes. Hocus and Pocus ran in circles around the fire.

Tony and Sissy did a terrible job of pretending they did not know the fire would be where it was. Their fake horror and pretend misunderstanding almost made Reggie puke. Reggie hated the dishonesty and Tony and Sissy reeked of lies. Reggie gave winks all around the group and he decided to join the band of liars.

"Oh my gosh!" Reggie screamed with all of the false enthusiasm he could gather. "They must have been here too," he said directly to 12UP which was massed before him.

They were silent. After the silence had gone on a moment too long, Mia nudged Sally with the tip of her elbow. Sally bobbed and said, "They were here." Sally looked off into space. Sally had seen the number of birdhouses around the campsite and knew she was "on." Sally's eyes followed the pattern of a spiral above her head until they came to rest upon a single point directly above her. With her eyes focused with a sublime intensity she said, "I can hear a voice." Sally pretended to listen and said to the group, "The voice wants us to form a circle around the fire. Hold hands," she said, still pretending to listen.

Looks passed between the members of 12UP and they all caught on to Sally's ruse. The group clasped hands and stood around the fire. Tony and Sissy stood back, confused.

"To the left," Sally called with her head to the sky. The group danced to an unheard music to the left. "To the right," Sally called. 12UP froze and then danced to the right. They were all into it and the dance was a rhythmic beauty. After circling the fire one complete turn, Sally fell from the group and lay face down and unmoving in the grass beyond the fire.

Reggie did not know if this was part of the act or real. He broke the circle and flew to her side on the ground.

"Do I deserve an Oscar?" Sally asked out of the side of her mouth to Reggie.

"You little..." Reggie began.

"Listen," Sally said. "Act like I am hurt."

Reggie leaned over Sally and whispered in her ear where she was the only one to hear. "Why are you so crazy?"

Sally just smiled, but did not respond for a moment as she acted like she was out for a long count. "Start to chant 'Blood,'" Sally said.

"What?" Reggie asked, truly confused.

"Start chanting the word 'blood,'" Sally directed again out of the corner of her mouth. "Cynthia's plan is going to work," Sally said.

"What!?" Reggie felt like he was going to faint.

"Cynthia told me her plan, and I know it is going to work," Sally confessed.

"Huh?" Reggie said again, about to fall over.

"Do it Reggie," Sally instructed. "The cameras are rolling."

Reggie popped up from Sally's ear and began a chant, "Blood. Blood. Blood..."

Reggie gave the eye to those around him and they picked up and continued the chant, once again circling the fire.

"Blood. Blood. Blood... Blood. Blood. Blood... Blood. Blood. Blood..."

Reggie eyed Sally on the ground as he circled around with the group chanting their new mantra. On one turn Sally gave Reggie the cut-throat sign meaning "stop."

He did. She stood and gave him a wink and the rest of the afternoon continued as if nothing out of the ordinary had happened. Tony and Sissy did not know what to say or think so they did not say anything at all.

"Um, uh," Tony said to the group, still trying to gather his thoughts about what had just occurred. "We are going to want to have a fire tonight, and I imagine this one might burn down pretty far in the next eight hours—so why don't you all gather some wood while Sissy and I set up camp."

"Is that weirdo Mr. George going to bring us our food again?" Deondra asked.

"No," Sissy answered. "There's not a road that leads to this site. The pioneer camp had some leftover food we will be using."

"Leftovers? At camp?" Charles gawked.

"Not leftovers like you would have at home, silly," Sissy answered. "They have cans of ravioli, stuff to make macaroni and cheese, marshmallows, beef jerky, and stuff like that."

"Oh," Charles said.

By the time Charles finished peppering Sissy with questions about the menu, Reggie and Sally were deep in the woods. They were not looking for wood, but a quiet place to talk out of sight from any birdhouses. When they were well into the woods and Sally could sense Reggie slowing down to stop, a wicked grin crossed her face.

Reggie was not amused. "When did you and Cynthia have time to talk?" he asked.

"When we split to go pack our backpacks she came to my cabin to talk."

"You didn't talk in the cabin, did you?" Reggie asked, worried. "We have a birdhouse in ours."

126

"No," Sally answered. "You know I'm smarter than that." She playfully punched Reggie in the arm. "We went to the girls' bathroom. No birdhouses in the bathhouses."

"Well, why did she tell you and not me?" Reggie asked.

"She was worried you would think her idea was stupid, and she wanted to know what I thought before she told the whole group."

"She was worried what I would think?"

"Yes," Sally answered. "You are pretty dense when it comes to girls," she said, raring her arm back acting as if she would punch him again. "She likes you and cares what you think."

A dazed look spread across Reggie's face. He looked as though he had just heard the secrets of the universe and his mind was boggled. Sally observed his reverie for as long as she could stand it and punched Reggie, causing him to snap out of his daze.

"So," Reggie began, "is it a good idea?"

"Better than you could ever imagine. She is having to pull some major strings here and call in some huge favors."

"Really?"

"Yes," Sally answered. "She has an older cousin named Emilio. Her dad helped him come to the United States from Mexico. Mr. Vargas helped him with money and helped him get his papers and stuff like that. Mr. Vargas also had Emilio live with them in their family home for two years and Cynthia said her dad sat down with Emilio every night after dinner at the kitchen table and taught him English."

"Holy cow," Reggie said.

"Yeah," Sally said, taking a deep breath. "So, Emilio feels pretty indebted to the Vargas family. Oh—Mr. Vargas also got him the job he has now—he drives a liquid tanker."

"What is a liquid tanker?" Reggie asked.

"It is a truck that carries thousands and thousands of gallons of liquid."

"Oh," Reggie said, "yeah, I have seen those on the highway. Sorry I asked, I know I am getting off the subject here."

"But you aren't," Sally answered him, smiling. "The liquid tanker truck is the centerpiece of our hoax."

"Huh?" Reggie uttered.

"Let's find a place to sit down for a minute, and let me rewind a bit."

Reggie and Sally found two giant rocks to perch upon, sitting comfortably across from one another. The Georgia pines blocked the persistent afternoon sun, and a light breeze unexpectedly trickled through the trees.

"So," Sally began, once they were settled. "Cynthia's cousin Emilio as I already told you is in the trucking business. He, of course has other friends in the business as well. Some of his trucker friends know he has connections to the camp here and told him about a secret job they have been hired to do. On Sunday, a group of flatbed truck drivers have been hired as well as a crane operator to lift and place large concrete structures into the creek. The flatbeds will be loaded with giant concrete barriers. The crane operator will lift them and place them in the water creating a temporary dam which will stop the water from going over the falls."

"Holy cow," Reggie said, visualizing the effort.

128

"Cynthia said that Emilio told her that his trucker friends had practiced this stunt earlier in the year when the camp was closed and it actually worked. They did it a couple of times to work out the timing and Emilio is sure they know exactly how to do it and make the falls stop at precisely eleven fifty-nine."

"When did she find all of this out?" Reggie asked.

"Last night," Sally answered. "Cynthia said they do all of this far enough upstream that we here at the camp will not see or hear a thing."

"And how does the liquid tanker truck come into play?" Reggie asked, curiously.

"Blood. Blood. Blood," Sally chanted, smiling with her wicked smile once again.

"Come on," Reggie said. "You are killing me here!"

"OK," Sally said, enjoying the moment. "After Emilio told her all of that other stuff last night, Cynthia remembered a prank Emilio had helped his boss do using the liquid tanker truck. She said Emilio filled the tanker with water and put a dye in the water that turned the water blood red. Emilio's boss had him fill the city's empty pool with the red water for Halloween. Supposedly the dye is harmless and will clear in a day's time. Do you know how much water a city pool holds?"

"What does any of that have to do with us?" Reggie asked.

"On Sunday night, Emilio is going to have the liquid tanker truck parked at the top of the falls. He is just going to pretend he was making a delivery, and his truck broke down. If Mr. Gary or anybody asks he will say the repair company will not be able to make it out until the morning."

"Oh my gosh," Reggie said, with his fingers in his mouth. "I think I might see where this is going."

"So, the liquid tanker truck will be parked on the road about thirty feet from the creek at the top of the falls. Emilio has a giant fifty foot hose that he will have attached to the truck and extending to the middle of the creek. Nobody will see it in the dark. At exactly midnight he will open the valve that lets all the water out of the truck. When he does, moments later it will look as though blood is running down the falls."

"Beautiful," Reggie said. "Beautiful."

Chapter 21

As they walked back to the pioneer camp with a few sticks in their hands, Reggie asked Sally if they should gather the rest of the group in the woods and tell them Cynthia's idea.

"No," Sally answered. "This is Cynthia's idea, and I think she should have the glory of revealing it."

"You're right," Reggie answered. "It is an awesome plan. How do we explain the blood chant if anyone asks?"

"We tell them to trust us, it is part of a plan which will be made known at our morning meeting tomorrow."

"Fair enough," Reggie said. "What do you think is going to happen tonight?"

"Who knows," Sally said laughing.

Back at camp the other kids looked at them suspiciously as they walked into the clearing thirty minutes later without any wood.

Noticing their stares, Sally said, "Reggie dropped his watch, the dimwit. We have been looking all over for it and finally found it."

"Yeah," Reggie said catching on, "my mom would have been so mad if I lost this watch—it was a birthday gift."

The other kids looked appeased.

Sally remembered an old fallen tree she had seen on the walk back and announced to the group, "Hey, there is a bunch of good wood over this way," she said, pointing the way she and Reggie had just come from. They all followed.

Standing on the tree, before they began breaking off the limbs, Sally said, "Cynthia has come up with a brilliant plan for Sunday night."

"What is it?" Bonnie asked.

"I want her to tell you in the morning," Sally answered. "And, I want to say I am sorry about springing the blood chant on all of you, but when I saw the fire, I thought of what Cynthia had said and I knew her plan would work. Most of you know that Reggie is my best friend—he didn't even know about it. I kind of sprung it on him and luckily he played along."

"Does he know about the plan?" Mia asked, her shyness showing once again.

"I do," Reggie answered. "I wanted to tell you all, but Sally made a good point to me when I asked her if we could. This is Cynthia's idea."

A loud crunching noise came rumbling through the woods, and the group froze. All of the kids crouched down ready for an attack or something weird to happen. Hocus and Pocus came running to where they were, and the kids all relaxed as the dogs found a spot and plopped down. As the dogs came to a rest the group tensed up again as they heard a low noise continue. The noise continued and grew louder. Once again, all the campers crouched, ready for the unexpected. A moment later, Cynthia walked over the hill.

As she approached, the group broke out with applause and cheers. A smile spread across her face and in Reggie's mind she walked in slow motion, her hair waving slowly from side to side, her hips swaying, her legs strutting, her eyes twinkling. Sally gave him a swift elbow to the side of his stomach. "You're about to drool on yourself," she said and laughed.

Reggie walked toward her and met her with a stupefied smile. His plan was to whisper in her ear that her plan was brilliant. Cynthia thought he was trying to

132

hug her and wrapped her arms around him. When Reggie felt her arms grip him and her hands placed against the small of his back he almost went limp with joy. Somehow, Reggie found the power to return the hug. As he hugged her he told her in her ear how wonderful her plan was. The intoxicating smell of her hair almost made him pass out. As they broke the embrace, Reggie stumbled back to the group like a drunk.

"We have found our fearless leader's weakness," Sally whispered to him. Reggie was so far up in the clouds he could not have cared what she said. Knowing he was going to be useless for a while, Sally took over.

"What are you doing here?" Sally asked when Cynthia was standing by the tree with the rest of the group.

"Sissy called camp from her cell phone and said they forgot to bring Mia's asthma medicine. There was nobody else available, and when I heard them talking about it I offered. I have been here a bunch of times before camp started when we were bringing up all the food for pioneer camp. I bet I have walked that trail twenty times."

"Thanks," Mia said. "Do you have to walk all the way back by yourself too?"

"No," Cynthia said. "My dad gave me the night off from work and told me to bring my sleeping bag and spend the night with you all. Is that alright?"

Reggie almost choked with surprise and glee. He actually bent over in a coughing fit.

"I have known Reggie for a long time," Sally said, "and I can actually translate what he just said which is, it is just fine with him." Sally flashed him an evil yet loving grin. "Instead of us all waiting until the morning, why don't you tell us all your fabulous plan now?"

The group nodded enthusiastically and Cynthia spoke. Reggie recovered and watched her with awe. Cynthia spoke with confidence, enthusiasm, and conviction. The group listened with wonder. They all loved her plan and were excited by the thought of it. They even came up with a finishing touch.

"We should get back to camp," Reggie said, fully recovered. "Sissy and Tony might wonder what we are doing out here. Everybody break off a few of these branches, and let's head back."

"What if something wacky happens tonight?" Benjamin asked.

Reggie looked out at the group seriously before answering. "Something wacky will happen tonight," he said. "I think we can count on that. As a group, as a family, we will deal with it. There is nothing they can do that will pull us apart or rattle us. We know what they are up to. We should expect anything and everything." Reggie thought as they all regrouped before returning to camp. "If Sally or I grab our shoulders and knock our elbows together it will be a sign to begin the chant. It may help us thwart off whatever they have in store for us tonight."

They all walked back to camp with armfuls of wood. Cynthia carried twice as much as everybody else. Reggie glided along behind her. Sally laughed her way behind Reggie.

Back at camp, Mia took her meds and the group separated the wood into piles as taught previously by Sissy. Sissy sat at a picnic table under a rugged pavilion peeling potatoes. She said she was making "Camp Fries." Sissy even promised ketchup. The kids all shuddered at the thought of unrefrigerated ketchup. Tony was nowhere to be seen.

Sissy told the kids that the rest of the afternoon until dinner would be free time—four hours total of free time. The campers usually had an hour or an hour and a half at the most. They were instructed to set up camp and to have fun. There were balls, Frisbees, gloves, and other things to play with in a small shed Sissy pointed out. Something was fishy. Fishy, fishy.

Since Cynthia was their guest, Reggie thought to ask her what she would like to do. She decided on soccer.

"Let's go see if there is a soccer ball in the shed," Reggie said.

As he and Cynthia walked toward the shed he wondered if he should try to kiss her once inside. Reggie took a few more steps and decided he would not like his first kiss to be inside a shed. Reggie was not yet a romantic, but an old shed did not appeal to his tender side.

Inside the shed they not only found a soccer ball, but they also found two goals. The shed happened to be quite big with two large barn doors at the back to get out the bigger items held inside. Reggie looked around the inside of the shed for birdhouses, a new habit he practiced constantly.

"Your idea is just awesome," he said, staring into Cynthia's eyes.

"I'm glad you like it," Cynthia answered. "I am so happy that your group has included me. Sometimes people treat me different."

"Why?" Reggie asked.

"Because I am from a different country. I speak another language. And I don't look like you."

"Yeah, you look better than me," Reggie joked. "You're beautiful."

Cynthia walked toward Reggie and Reggie wondered in that split second if his first kiss would happen in a shed after all. In the next moment, they heard screaming outside the shed. Both of their heads turned in the direction of the noise. Realizing something was terribly wrong they ran out of the shed.

The screaming came from the woods just outside of camp. The banging sound of gunfire filled the air as well as the sound of terrified men screaming. Reggie looked around to see where the rest of the group stood. His eyes searched the grounds and finally found them under the pavilion used for cooking and eating. Tony and Sissy were nowhere to be found. Surprise, surprise. From the sound of the screaming, Reggie could tell that there was not enough time to make it under the pavilion with the rest of the group before whoever was coming reached the field.

Just as he thought this, three men ran into view. Each of the men wore black and white striped prison uniforms. One of the men had shackles broken and hanging from both of his legs. The other men had hands that were still cuffed, but somehow they had managed to get their hands and arms in front of their bodies instead of behind their backs. Each of the men had nappy beards and dirty looking hair. They *looked* like criminals.

As they sprinted across the field, the sound of gunfire once again filled the air. The men in prison garb exited the field on the opposite side and entered the woods again. As they did, a group of men in police uniforms came running into view. Some of the men were brandishing firearms and occasionally for some reason firing them in the air. Reggie and Cynthia watched the group of cops run straight toward the rest of their group. The cops stopped in front of them for a few moments, obviously asking the kids which way the group of ruffians ran. Reggie and Cynthia observed a lot of pointing. Most of the kids were pointing in the direction in which they had actually disappeared. Sally was pointing in the opposite direction and Reggie smiled.

Unable to speak, Cynthia put her arm around Reggie's waist. Reggie almost passed out with feelings. Another gunshot filled the air as Cynthia turned her head to face Reggie. Reggie saw a mass of bodies running and forgot them as he focused his gaze upon Cynthia. Eye to eye. Brown eyes to blue. His lips touched hers. A moment burned in their minds forever as Reggie's heart boiled to a never before degree. Cynthia would forever be the absolute by which all other girls were measured.

The beauty shattered when Pocus grabbed the edge of Reggie's pants with her teeth and pulled. Reggie wondered if she was trying to protect them. Reggie looked to the pavilion again and saw Hocus standing guard. Leaving the equipment shed, Reggie grabbed a bucket filled with croquet balls thinking they might be used as protective projectiles if the prisoners came back and if they were for real.

As Reggie and Cynthia joined the rest of the group under the pavilion, the dogs stood together with the campers behind them. The dogs both standing statue still, moved only their heads side to side, baring their teeth.

"Where are Tony and Sissy?" Reggie asked.

"Gone," Sally answered. "Whenever something weird happens they either seem to disappear or they're not allowed to talk about it."

"This one might be real," Reggie suggested.

"Right," Sally said, sarcastically.

"Look at the way the dogs are acting," Reggie offered. "Who thinks this one is real?" Everybody except Sally and Charles raised their hands.

"I've always had dogs," Deondra said, "and dogs know what is going on."

"Yeah," Charles said, "but dogs can also be trained to do certain things. They brought us to camp on the first day! Hocus and Pocus tracked Mr. George to the lake on the night of the first campout. They were running in a circle around the campfire when we got here today!"

Before the argument could continue, they heard the screaming voices again. Instinctively, Reggie grabbed the bucket of croquet balls and handed them out. Even Sally and Charles took one, they said they would play along to whatever Reggie had in mind.

"OK," Reggie said. "If the prisoners pass us I will quickly count to three. On three we will all throw our croquet balls. Aim at their heads. If they are real prisoners we will hopefully knock them out. If they are actors, they will be sorry they messed with us."

Some of the campers smiled and others clinched with nerves. The voices became louder, and the sound of sticks snapping underfoot rushed through the woods. As the black and white uniforms appeared in brief flashes through the trees the campers gripped the croquet balls and readied to launch them in an aerial assault.

The three men in prison garb broke through the trees. Reggie eyed the path in which they were headed. It would take them, he estimated, directly in front of the pavilion.

"Get ready," he announced to the group. They all cocked their arms back, ready to fire. When the prisoners were ten yards from passing in front, Reggie began

138

counting. "One, two, three." On three the men were directly in front of them, and ten heavy croquet balls were hurled at their heads.

The men dropped like they had been shot. As soon as they hit the ground, Hocus and Pocus were on top of them barking and frothing madly in a manner the kids did not know they were capable of exhibiting. Puffing and out of breath the cops busted out of the woods and stopped dead in their tracks, amazed at what laid before them.

"Call off your dogs!" one of the police officers shouted.

"Come here Hocus," Reggie yelled. "Come here Pocus." The dogs ran to Reggie. Ruffling their heads lovingly he said, "You are such a good girl," and "you are such a good boy." The dogs panted with pride.

Two of the police officers cuffed the prisoners correctly and one spoke into a walkie-talkie, giving his location to the party on the other end. Two of the prisoners were still knocked unconscious, and one began to stir with a slight moan.

Once the officers had caught their breath they looked around and all at once seemed to notice the croquet balls surrounding the prisoners.

The officer who they later learned was named Richard began laughing as he put two and two together. "Did you all...?" he started to ask.

"Yes we did," Reggie said quickly, not sure if they were going to be in trouble or not.

"Thanks," he said. "Maybe you knocked some sense into them."

From the bushes and trees they heard what sounded like motors. They previously were told there was not a road leading to this site. Reggie looked to Officer

Richard and he told Reggie and the group that what they were hearing was the sound of four-wheelers coming to retrieve the prisoners.

From the other direction the campers heard additional noises. It sounded as if someone was hightailing it through the woods blindly, running into every low hanging branch and tripping over every root and rock in the forest. Tony and Sissy sprang from the trees like clumsy deer and stopped in front of the downed prisoners in the same manner as the police officers.

"Thank goodness you got them," Sissy said to the officers. She was out of breath.

"We didn't get them," Officer Richard announced. "These kids did," he said, pointing his finger to the group of campers.

"How?" Tony asked, his face showed astonishment.

At this point Reggie and all the other campers were watching and taking in the scene with careful eyes and ears. They tried with each word, each gesture, and every single bit of eye contact to determine if this was real or not.

"I don't know exactly how they did it," Officer Richard said, "but my guess is they surprised them with a face full of croquet balls. Knocked them clean out. Those balls are awfully heavy."

Three four-wheelers pulled into camp towing tiny caged trailers that looked like oversized dog kennels. Without delay the additional officers stuffed the prisoners into them without any care whatsoever and hauled them off, going back the same direction from which they had come. Officer Richard shook hands all around and thanked the campers for their bravery. With his thanks expressed, he gave an order to the other two men with him and walked off after the caravan of four-wheelers with the men following behind.

As soon as they were out of sight, the eyes and attention of each camper turned to Tony and Sissy. The campers did not want to give up what they knew to be going on but they also were torn with the feeling that they might have escaped from some real danger.

"You all were so brave," Sissy said. "Let me explain what happened." Nobody said a word. "I carry an emergency beeper on my belt at all times. We were told that it would only be used in the event of a major emergency. After I called for Mia's medication my phone died. When you guys went out to get firewood I told Tony about it and he was concerned of the possibility of us needing help in the middle of the night or something else happening where we needed to contact camp. So, he decided to head back to camp to get his cell phone which he said was charging in his cabin. Twenty or so minutes later my emergency beeper went off and since I knew everything was fine here, I thought something terrible must be happening in camp." Sissy paused to look around at the campers. They were all dialed into her story, so she continued. "I did not want to scare any of you or have you worried, so I just quietly slipped away. Once I was out of sight I ran the entire way back to camp. I ran so fast that I actually arrived about two minutes after Tony who had been walking briskly. We went straight to Mr. Gary's office and were appalled when he told us the emergency was escaped prisoners near the woods of the pioneer camp. Without saying a word we ran back, thinking the worst the entire time." Sissy looked around at the group again and said, "I am so relieved." She broke down and cried like a baby.

The campers did not know what to think. To believe or not to believe. That was the question. Nobody that night had any answers.

Chapter 22

Sunday morning began to slowly bloom. The big day—or night, had finally arrived. Eleven fifty-nine could not come soon enough. Reggie awoke before the sun as usual and peered over to where he knew Cynthia slept. As she slept, her hair crossed her face in a messy maze and he thought he had never seen anything so precious in his entire life. Reggie felt so many things at this moment. He felt his crush for Cynthia. It pressed his heart and tugged at it all at the same time. He felt fantastic and like he would throw up at the same time. *This must be love*, he thought.

He then plopped his head back onto his pillow and stared into the fleeting stars feeling what he knew was big and just as important as love, leadership. *People needed leaders,* Reggie thought. *How did I become one?* Reggie puzzled at the thought for a moment and decided it was not important how he had become one; it was now important what he did with his leadership.

The Sunday that began as a bloom began to flower. Cynthia woke up. She sat up and looked at Reggie. Reggie snapped from his thoughts and smiled. He blew her a kiss and Cynthia reached up and pretended to catch it. She placed it on her cheek and returned the smile and a blown kiss of her own.

They both climbed out of their sleeping bags as the others slept and walked toward the woods.

After their morning salutations, Reggie said, "Are you going to hear from your truck driver cousin today?"

"I am," Cynthia answered. "He is supposed to call mid-morning and bring the truck late afternoon. He

143

doesn't want to pretend to break down too early in case someone calls in a wrecker or gets suspicious."

"Good," Reggie answered, thinking.

"What are you worried about?" Cynthia asked, reading Reggie's face.

"I'm worried about the group," Reggie answered. "Are they going to be able to hold it together? To not give away what we know. To pull it all off?"

"I think it all depends," Cynthia answered.

"Depends on what?" Reggie asked.

"You," Cynthia said. "It depends on you."

An hour later the entire group packed and readied to head back to camp. As they began to walk back down the trail to camp, Reggie thought of what Cynthia had said. He could either take the situation as a burden or a challenge. It took only a few steps for Reggie to make his decision. He would accept the challenge. *Bring it on,* he thought.

Back at camp they deposited their backpacks and other items in the cabins and headed to breakfast in the dining hall. They were the last group to be seated, and when they entered the hall the campers inside stood and gave them a standing ovation. News had travelled fast about their apprehension of the three criminals. The group did not know what to feel, so they looked to Reggie and took his lead. They nodded humbly and tried to ignore the attention as they ate their breakfasts.

Reggie knew from this moment that they would all hold it together and pull off their plan. They could have basked in the glory of catching criminals, but they did not. They looked to him for direction and acted as he did. In this moment he felt the enormous power of leadership. Reggie flushed with pride. Most of all he felt the weight of responsibility. *I will be a good leader,* Reggie thought. *I will be a good leader.* Thinking this thought, feeling this thought, and living this thought, the day passed with ease.

Whispers about the falls made their way around camp during the day and faded as evening fell. By the time the bell for dinner rang it seemed as though everybody had made up their minds as to whether they would try to slip out of their cabins to watch the falls and what might or might not happen. Reggie knew some of the conversations must have been caught by the birdhouse cameras, and he pictured Mr. Gary and the crew giddy with their final stunt.

At nine fifty-seven p.m., Tony snored loud enough to hear outside the cabin. The boys, all in black crept from their beds and headed to meet the girls. Sissy, still exhausted from running up and down the mountain the night before crashed before the girls could even get all dressed in black. As Sissy slept, the girls pulled on their dark clothing. They knew she wouldn't hear and giggled as they left the cabin.

The group met at their secret spot. It was the first time they had met there after dark, and the entire atmosphere of the meeting place changed. Cynthia borrowed some candles from the dining hall and passed one to each person. They stood in a circle and she handed Reggie a lighter. He lit his candle and turned to his left to light Sally's. Reggie then turned to his right and lit Cynthia's candle. The light spread around the circle, and the atmosphere changed again.

"This is our big night," Reggie began. His stomach fluttered with nerves and adrenaline. "This summer has been one to remember forever." Reggie looked at all of their faces and smiles passed back and forth. "We have one more task to complete together to show these television people that we will not be messed with. I have a feeling we will not be the only campers there tonight. Here is what we will do before and after the falls stop..." Reggie explained a simple plan and the kids discussed the what ifs of the plan.

At precisely eleven fifty-two the members of 12UP approached the falls. Powerful lights lit the falls brilliantly. *Showtime*, Reggie thought. Reggie could tell by slight movements that there were other kids in the surrounding woods. Just how many, he did not know. The members of 12UP assembled in a semicircle around the falls, kneeling on the sandy beach, holding hands. It looked as though they were about to perform some sort of ritual.

One by one, two by two, three by three, and then in masses, the kids hiding in the woods came out from the shadows. They lined up behind the members of 12UP in semicircle fashion, taking their lead and following suit. Each member of 12UP had the verse Reggie had devised memorized and whispered it over their shoulder to the person behind them. "This is all a game. Don't be scared. Follow the lead. Pass it on." The word quickly spread, and Reggie checked his watch. It read eleven fifty-eight. On his cue, the group began to pass the message again, just to make sure all of those in attendance got it right. "This is all a game. Don't be scared. Follow the lead. Pass it on." As Reggie glanced over his shoulder to deliver the verse a

146

second time his eyes widened at the group which had assembled. He estimated that at least three quarters of the camp must have been kneeling behind them.

Mr. Gary sat under the barn-hall in the control both. It was not his usual behavior to enter the control booth at night, but this was the moment that would cap the show he had envisioned. A show that would capture all of the genius he felt he deserved.

He sat, drinking coffee, watching the monitors. Mr. Gary expected to see the kids scared out of their minds. Minds blown with the enormity of the falls stopping. As he was about to sip his brew he noticed the kids in a semicircle around the falls. Mr. Gary stared into the television monitors offering different views of the moment at hand. Each view showed the group holding hands, kneeling around the bottom of the falls. He could not believe the amount of kids the monitors showed. Curiosity prickled the back of his neck and the top of his shoulders as he wondered why they were kneeling and holding hands.

At eleven fifty-nine, as promised, the falls stopped. Mr. Gary watched, smiling with anticipation. He wanted to see the kids lose their minds with misunderstanding. It did not happen. For a minute they did not even move.

Reggie watched the seconds tick away on his watch carefully. He and Cynthia's cousin Emilio had synchronized their watches. At exactly midnight he began the chant. "Blood. Blood. Blood... Blood. Blood. Blood... Blood. Blood. Blood..."

Before Mr. Gary could even begin to form an idea of what might be happening, the blood red water began to drip over the falls. It began as a trickle and quickly became rapids of red. As the blood red water poured over the falls the group continued to hold hands as if nothing was wrong. The chant continued. Mr. Gary watched the monitors and freaked. What he was seeing could not be real. He yelled at the people working the booth. He ran out of the booth and toward the falls. The kids held their pose and continued the chant. "Blood. Blood. Blood... Blood. Blood. Blood... Blood. Blood. Blood..."

As the last of the blood red water descended the falls, Mr. Gary arrived before them with some of his staff on his heels. Mr. Gary's eyes were wild with confusion, and he was tugging at his hair with fear. His arms shook uncontrollably.

Reggie decided to do the chant one more time and gave his next secret signal to his group by clapping as he lead the chant this last time. "Blood. Blood. Blood... Blood. Blood. Blood... Blood. Blood. Blood..." As previously discussed in the secret meeting spot, once they did this they would begin a new and final chant. And they did, with all of the campers behind them doing just as they had asked and following their lead. "Watch Camp TV, Watch Camp TV, Watch Camp TV."

Reggie had figured out during the previous night's unrest that Camp Timber View was the cover for what he thought must be the reality show's name—Camp TV. He had always thought the "T" and the "V" in all of the free merchandise they were given was drawn too big. It was on the shirts, the hats, the pants, you name it. Wherever the words Camp Timber View were written, the "T" and the "V" were always bigger.

The campers continued their new chant as the regular water from the falls began again. "Watch Camp TV, Watch Camp TV, Watch Camp TV."

Mr. Gary's expression turned from terrified to baffled to amused. His mind did a thousand flips and finally landed on Reggie. Their eyes met and Reggie smiled. Mr. Gary knew he had been outdone and surprisingly, he loved it.

Mr. Gary summoned Reggie to his office where they told each other their secrets. Reggie knew most of his except the bit with the prisoners. To Reggie's surprise that was real, but all caught on camera. Reggie told Mr. Gary about Emilio, the hidden recorder, and their secret meeting spot. They laughed like old friends as they told their tales.

As Reggie and Mr. Gary held their meeting, Sally held one below the falls. She thanked the other campers for playing along and told them everything she knew about the camp and the pranks and the birdhouses. Nobody saw their beds until about three in the morning. The campers that were already asleep were awakened and let in on the news.

The following morning, just after breakfast, the families arrived to pick up all of the campers from camp. The summer was over. Reggie exchanged addresses with the other members of 12UP. He knew he would see Sally on a day to day basis, but he was unsure what to do about Cynthia. He didn't just want her address, email, or phone number.

Before the parents were let in the gate, Reggie went to see Cynthia at the dining hall. He thanked Mr. and

Mrs. Vargas for such a wonderful summer. They hugged him warmly with unusual twinkles in their eyes. He had tears in his. He and Cynthia hugged as her parents watched.

"I'll miss you," Reggie said, aware of the fact that her parents were hovering so close. Cynthia returned the sentiment. "Can I write you letters?" Reggie asked.

"I would like that," Cynthia answered. "We are moving to a new town."

"Oh," Reggie answered. "OK."

"It's called Alpharetta."

"Are you serious?" Reggie exclaimed.

"Yes," Cynthia answered, confused by Reggie's excitement.

"That's where I live."

They both looked at Mr. and Mrs. Vargas who were smiling knowingly. Reggie and Cynthia hugged again with excitement.

The final ceremony was held on the ball field. There were cameras everywhere—no longer in disguise. The campers learned all of the secrets Reggie had learned the night before in Mr. Gary's office. Their parents had known all along what was going on. The show had been on the air all summer. The final episode had aired live the night before and the ratings were incredible.

As the ceremony ended, Reggie found his family. He hugged his mom and dad and they told him how proud they were of him. As they finished with their praise and stood back, Reggie saw his older brother Ronald standing behind. Ronald had never been a big fan of Reggie. To him, Reggie was just an annoying person who interrupted his television shows and his life in general.

"Reggie," Ronald said, with a glee Reggie had never seen before directed his way. "I watched you all summer," Ronald confessed, without shame. Ronald's eyes were full of stars. To him, Reggie was now a television star. "You are so awesome, Reggie," Ronald said.

Reggie looked around. Mr. Gary had been standing near and witnessed Ronald's praise.

"Is this a new show of yours?" Reggie asked Mr. Gary, joking. "My older brother actually thinks I did something cool?"

Mr. Gary shook his head saying no.

Reggie smiled. Ronald thought he was cool.

Well I'll be darned, Reggie thought. *I'll be darned.*

20326099R00092

Made in the USA
Middletown, DE
23 May 2015